T0354970

Lacey MacClean

and the Last Human

Lacey
MacClean
and the Last Human

The Final Installment
in the
"Josephine Daudry" Trilogy

Kevin Bailey

 iUniverse®

LACEY MACCLEAN AND THE LAST HUMAN
THE FINAL INSTALLMENT IN THE "JOSEPHINE DAUDRY" TRILOGY

iUniverse books may be ordered through booksellers or by contacting:

iUniverse
1663 Liberty Drive
Bloomington, IN 47403
www.iuniverse.com
844-349-9409

ISBN: 978-1-6632-6869-3 (sc)
ISBN: 978-1-6632-6870-9 (e)

Library of Congress Control Number: 2024923885

Print information available on the last page.

iUniverse rev. date: 11/14/2024

INTRODUCTION

Lacey MacClean and the Last Human, is the last chapter in the *Josephine Daudry Trilogy.* The name, Lacey MacClean was the spark that started me writing Josephine's story in my first book titled, *Josephine Daudry.* In the book, Lacey was a fictitious character that Josephine (Josy) thought up, first as a new name for herself and then as a person she aspired to be. Eventually, Josy came into her own and did not change her name. But that character, Lacey MacClean, continued to come back into Josy's life. So, at the end of the second book of the trilogy, *Sometimes Love Lands Sideways,* I added into the story a phone call from Lacey, from the future. Why? Well, I wondered to myself, *What if Lacey was real? What if she called Josy? From where and when? And most importantly, how would that work in this story?* So, here is my answer to those questions.

Thinking about the future is a common theme among writers, so the concept is nothing new. An apocalyptic dystopia with only a handful of humans left; you know the story. But I thought of a little twist; what if these few souls could talk to someone from a hundred or more years ago? With the advent of AI, it is already being explored in businesses. But for my story, it is not as much about business, as it is survival.

I hope that you enjoy this book, the last in the trilogy. And if you have not read the first two books yet, please do. It would be helpful to have the full background to this story.

The first two books relied heavily on my life and my family for fictionalized content. The storyline was original, but events from my life were inserted with obvious dramatic license. This book, however, can only draw on the general human experience and reflect the many published visions of the future that I have encountered. But mainly, I let the story take me on its own journey with this character, Lacey MacClean.

Kevin Bailey   October 2024

CONTENTS

CHAPTER 1

Lacey and Her Goat

DARKNESS IS ABOUT TO GIVE WAY. THE SUN IS JUST OVER THE HORIZON casting a black shadow over Càrn Dearg, the mountain to the west. The air is clean, with foggy droplets providing coolness to the face of Lacey MacClean as she flies down the highland road into the valley. She is trying to beat the sun to her destination, a cottage built in the side of a hill, a cave, really. She rides her Cyclone, a kinetically powered tri-wheeled bike. Like the old flywheel toys from hundreds of years ago…it revs up and then goes, but with one difference. The flywheel has a geo-magnet. Its frequency is set to the same as the earth's magnetic core, so that once started, it will turn as long as it is engaged. To shut it off…a polar opposite magnet is employed… The bike's rear dual wheels are close together, but still provide more stability than a two-wheeler. The bike is aerodynamic…sleek and fun to ride…fast.

Lacey wears a coat that is reflective and provides some protection from the harmful rays of the sun. It covers her all the way down to her boots. It is long and flies in the wind as she rides along. But it is heavy enough so that it doesn't flutter and still keeps her covered. She also has a hat made of the same protective material. It has a towel like tail to cover her neck area. The whole get up makes her look like some kind of silver bird, soaring on a thermal, flying down the road.

She stops on a hill to watch the sun rise, then she pedals hard to build up the flywheel's energy letting off the brake when she's ready…the bike takes off…fast…0 to 40kph in 7 seconds a few more pedals and she accelerates to 70kph and then even faster, finally sliding to a halt at a door that leads into her home.

This is her morning routine, around Loch Insh and home again. *I love this place, this…this…Scotland, I only wish I could stay outside longer.* She thinks to herself. This is all still new to her…the name…the place…the emptiness.

Lacey is new to herself too. Though she has been self-aware since… she draws a blank because she really can't remember when. She doesn't know how she came to be. One day she just was. She keeps a journal. She writes to remember…hopefully…something beyond the present. She wonders how she knows the things she does. *It's like I'm always watching myself as I do things. How do I know how to garden, cook, and milk my goat. When did I get here? How do I know my name? Where is everyone else? Am I alone? What does my dream mean? So many questions…no answers.*

★ ★ ★

As the sun rises higher, the mirrors now engage on the top of the hill above her cave. They reflect light through a system of filters and mirrors to let only good light down into her cave home. Beautifully built, adorned with murals on solid rock walls the cave is functional and yet homey. The entrance looks like a cottage from pictures in books Lacey has. Tales of another time, she guesses. The pictures show people, lots of people. *Where did everyone go?* She wonders as she reads and wishes she could understand how she came to be.

Looking out over the valley, Lacey can see beyond it to a vast land. It looks as barren as the land around her. There are no colorful plants or flowers like she has in her indoor garden. She has tried to grow some outside, but they just wither and die. Grass grows outside, but not much else. She works dirt and mixes it with compost and that provides her a fertile soil for her indoor garden which draws light from the mirrors. There is a stream in the lower part of the cave and with it she has plenty of water. She produces just enough food for her needs but not much more. If it wasn't for the indoor garden, her first winter would have been her undoing.

The only good thing about the winter, was that she could do more exploring during the day because the sun was so low in the sky. But the icy roads made it tough to get much traction, until she found a feature on the Cyclone; a tire pressure pump. Which let her lower the pressure and make the tires softer for better traction. Not going so fast helped too. A few spills into the snow and hard icy ground taught her that lesson.

These spring evenings she can also explore when the sun is setting, but the time is always limited. Every evening she looks out over the same valley and sees the land beyond. She wants to explore it, but each time she tries to ride out to see more of the land she comes to a sudden halt. There is something deep inside her that makes her stop. She turns around and heads back without understanding exactly why. There is always an overwhelming feeling of sudden dread and thoughts, like, *It's almost time to eat, or, I need to tend my garden, or, the sun is going down, and I don't want to be caught out in the dark.*

She has tried to ignore these thoughts, but the next thing she knows she's on her way back and by then she figures it really is time to go home. *Home, what does that mean when I'm all alone?* She wonders.

★ ★ ★

As Lacey looks at herself in a mirror, she sees a young woman with long red hair, green eyes and light complexion. She wonders about the wall murals. Painted on them are trees and mountains and brooks. But no people or flowers. *Why? I see all that in my books, why are there none outside my door? And why are there all these animals in my books, but all I have, is this goat?*

Lacey reads her books a lot as she sits by her window. She likes books about funny things, but lately has been reading more serious books as well. She reads about families, mothers and sons, fathers and daughters. But she has no one like that and can't remember any.

"Where's my mom…my dad…I have no brother or sister, all I got is you…you…old goat. And where did you come from? Same place as me, I guess. Anyway, thanks for being here, and thanks for the milk…uhm…hey, what's your name? I don't remember it. Well, I guess I can call you whatever I like. Let see…how about…hmm, I don't know any names for goats. I don't even know any names except for my own and the few in these books.

Lacey picks up a children's book and opens it. "There is a dog named Spot…you don't have any spots." She tosses that book aside and picks up another. "There is a cat named…aah…(she flips through the pages) no name…it's just in a hat; I don't get that. But there are no goats." Looking in another book, she says, "There is a girl named Nelly. Nelly? Do you like that name?"

The goat bleats. "No? Yeah, I agree. That's not the right name for you." Lacey keeps flipping through different books. "Well, let's see, how about…Beatrice? That's a cow…you do kinda have the cows colors." The goat turns away. "Okay, don't be like that. I will find you a name. It may take some time, but I will; I promise."

Lacey continues looking through her books. She has a shelf with plenty of them. There are math books and other books for learning about cooking and farming. There are books about anatomy, philosophy, poems, and romance, along with the children's stories. She doesn't remember reading them, but when it comes to her work she wonders if that's how she knows how to garden and do everything else. *Why can't I remember? I remember my name. I know how to take care of myself; provide for myself. What am I missing?* She wonders.

One day Lacey said to the goat, "How about this? On my ride this morning I found a rusty old sign with names on it. I could hardly to read them but I think the top said, Dalwhin…with a rusty 'e'. And under it was another name, Kingussie. Should I call you one of those names? Dalwhin…win..Winnie? Or maybe Gussie…I can't call you King Gussie…how about Queen Gussie? Nah…just Winnie I think. Winnie it is." That seemed to satisfy the goat as she came near and head butted Lacey. "Now, how about some milk Winnie my lady…I won't call you an old goat anymore, and why did I call you old? I don't even know how old you are, or myself for that matter. Anyway, you have a name now."

*   *   *

After breakfast she tended her chores and then sat down to read. On the wall beside the books was a map of the Scottish Highlands. She could see there was a lot more to the country side than what she had explored. But it was not a detailed map. There were no road signs or names on it. It just showed the terrane of the mountains, valleys, rivers and lochs. She was reading a story about a family and had drifted off into a light sleep. As she awoke she found herself staring at the map. And then it occurred to her. *If there is a book about families, then the person who wrote this must have known a family. All of these books had to come from someone who experienced what they wrote. Or at least based the story on reality. Right? So where was it? And where is everyone? They had to live somewhere. I can't be the only one. This can't be the only cave. I have to break out of this place and get to the other end of the valley. I have to set my mind to it. I will start out in the dark and then ride on through sunrise. I will ride down that big hill and I won't stop until I get passed where the river meets the road. Then I can, hopefully, find cover or a cave to stay in until sundown, and then keep going. I can pack food, and water. But will I be able to ignore the feelings, and will the summer's longer daylight allow me to get there? I don't dare wait for fall because I don't know how long it will take me and I don't want to get caught in winter.*

Lacey has had daydreams about riding down into the lowlands, getting to where she could see what is there, but, as she envisions this, she suddenly feels lost and hears her name, "Lacey!" Startled, she is pulled out of her daydream. This, plus the feelings of needing to get back home always keeps her afraid of trying to ride into the lowlands. But now, Lacey is determined. *At least, I think I am, I hope I am.* She thinks. But then she sighs as she remembers the nightmare she has had over and over. She shakes her head, gets up and starts some water for tea.

*   *   *

Lacey drew a replica of the map and began putting names to the geography. "Sunrise Mountain," the Valley Road, the Road River, because it followed the road until it crossed it. That was her goal for the first leg of her journey. Then she would continue down that road into the unknown. She rigged up a bag to carry her food, water and extra clothes, and the extra coat to shield her from the sun. She planned for days and then it occurred to her, *What about Winnie?* "I can't go without you. And besides who will milk you while I'm gone? I've got to take you with me; but how?"

A few days later Lacey was on her morning ride and decided to turn down a dirt path to explore. *I won't go too far.* She thought. As she rode down the path it led to a steep decline. She stopped and looked over the edge of the hollow and saw shapes sticking up out of the dust and dirt. But then, she could see the sun was already breaking over the ridge, so she decided there just wasn't enough time. *I will come back early tomorrow and get down there.* She promised herself.

The next morning she went back and had brought a garden shovel. Digging into a jutting mound of dust and dirt she hit metal. The clang made her jump at first. But she kept moving the shovel to get under it. Slowly she dug around it and was able to leverage the shovel to push it up. It was an old bucket, rusty but no holes. Lacey shook out the dirt and saw it could be useful. She began digging around to see what else she could find. Something big was under the area where she found the bucket. She dug and dug but was not getting close to the bottom. She would have to come back.

A few days of digging finally revealed the object. It was about a half meter wide and one and a half meters long, and about a meter tall. She remembered seeing this in a book. It was a feeder for cows and other animals. As she brushed it off she had a thought. *This is big enough for Winnie. But I need wheels. How could I make that work? And how can I get this back to my cave? I can't hold it and ride at the same time.*

★ ★ ★

Back home, Lacey dove into her books looking for ideas. She saw what was called motorbikes with sidecars. That looked like a good idea, but how to attached it to her bike, was the question. She went back to the hollow and dug up more stuff. Most of it was worthless but she did find a snowboard. After looking at if for a bit, she put the feeder trough on it and fastened it as best she could with twine she brought from her cave. Carrying it up the hill to her Cyclone was unwieldy, but that turned out to be the easy part. Trying to tow it behind the bike was useless. It kept falling to one side and coming loose. She didn't get far down the path before getting off the bike, sitting down and giving out a big sigh. "Phooey," She said. It was the only thing she could think of saying. She read it in a children's book and it felt good to say it. She didn't understand why, but it felt good, so she said it again. "Phooey," and again, only louder, "Phooey!"

Then she thought maybe there was another...whatever it is. *I know what it is, but I can't remember what it's called. I will look for it in my books.* Back down the hill she began digging around looking for another snowboard to use to keep the trough stable, but then, she realized it was past sunrise. The hollow she was in gave her more time than usual, but now, she could feel the itching on her head and arms. She quickly put the reflective coat back on, but it was not enough protection in the full sun of daytime. She left her shovel and hurried up the hill to her Cyclone but as she got higher the sun's rays became too much. She could feel her skin burning. She was now beginning to panic. There was no place to hide here. She looked around, trying to think as the burning was getting worse. She then screamed, "Phooey!" She fell to her knees and thought this was it. But then she remembered, she had a shovel. She went back to it and found the large hole she had dug to get the feeding trough out of. She laid down in the hole, and used the shovel to cover herself. Her coat had a water pouch and small hose to suck water on her rides. She quickly detached it and stuck it through the dirt to get air. There she lay, waiting and hoping this would work. The mid-day winds would be coming and could blow her covering right off exposing her again. *Why didn't I bring that trough back down with me? I could have used it.*

She thought. But then she realized she had to really make plans for her and Winnie to hide from the sun if she was ever going to get to the lowlands; that is if she could survive until sundown today. She sighed as she said it once more, "Phooey!"

The winds weren't bad that day and Lacey survived to make it home just after dusk. She put salve on her arms and forehead and checked herself to see if she had any lesions. She went right to sleep. Winnie bleated at her, but seeing she was not responding she went and sat down in her pen. Lacey was out, but the nightmare came again.

★ ★ ★

It was the same dream every time. Lacey would find herself in a long hallway with brilliant white walls, ceiling and floors. They were luminescent and glassy, At the end of the corridor she could see another going to the left or right, and she could hear her name being called. "Lacey," the voice would call. It sounded like a child but she could not tell if it might be the whisper of an adult. She would begin walking toward the corner as the sound was getting fainter. "I'm coming," Lacey would say as she began to trot. Every time she reached the corner and went around it, she would find another corridor just like the one she left. No one there, just the voice calling her name. She would go from a trot to a run and then faster to keep up with the calling. She could hear her name being called louder and louder and so the faster and faster she ran, turning every corner to the left or right whichever direction the sound was coming from. Barely making the turn around the corners, crashing into the walls, falling and getting up to run again, she chased the sound of her name. Finally, the sound volume would stabilize. It would stop moving away. Lacey would slow down and come cautiously to the corner. She would stop and wait for the sound of her name. "Lacey," the voice would say, only calmer than before. *Is it my mom?* Lacey would wonder, and then start to go around the corner to see, but as she did, the corner was gone. She was standing in front of a white wall. She heard the voice again, "Lacey," and then she would wake up, exhausted and confused.

* * *

Lacey woke up from the nightmare this time with Winnie licking her face. "Eew! Don't do that Winnie." Lacey said as she pushed the goat away and got up. "I need a bath. But yes, I will feed you first. So stop butting my leg, you old…umm, yeah, I said I wouldn't call you that anymore. But if you keep butting me and licking me, I may change my mind." Winnie bleated, and went into her pen and stood by her big dish waiting for food. Winnie would eat just about anything. So there was nothing in the cave that had not been gnawed on. Her food, which was anything from left overs to grass and grain, was stored up high in a cleft in the rock wall. Lacey dutifully fed the goat and then went to bathe in the cave stream. The cool water made her arms feel better. There were some burns there but none on her forehead. It could have been worse. *I would have never thought of burying myself to hide from the sun, but that could come in handy. I need to have a plan for that when we are on the road,* She thought.

"I'm going back to the hollow," Lacey said to Winnie, who just ignored her as she chewed away. "See you later, but not so late, like yesterday." Riding to the hollow that morning, Lacey thought about ways to attach the trough to her bike. *Even if I can drag it back home, how can I attach wheels to it and then to the bike? Twine won't last on a road trip. I need something much sturdier. There has to be something in the hollow. I wish the back two wheels were farther apart. The bikes' wheels are not wide enough to put the trough in between them. It was designed for speed not work. I guess because of the sun. Why is the light so bad anyway?*

* * *

Days of digging turned into weeks. The fall was already blooming, and winter would be coming, and Lacey wanted to make the trip before the cold and bitter gale forced winds came. One day she found a wagon. It had no wheels but it had a handle. The body was rusted and not much good but the handle and axels might be useful. *I still need at least two wheels.* She thought as she dug some more.

Then it happened. The last push of the shovel as the sun was rising, she heard a thud. She kept pushing the shovel against the object and found it was round. This was a small bit of hope that had let her down before. As she poked around she remembered the weird oval porcelain ring she found. It looked a little like a yoke for a cow. But porcelain? Then there was the large can that she made use of at home for more compost. And many other round things that weren't wheels. She kept digging though, and finally freed this new object. As she pulled it out of the dirt, she thought, *Ahh, two wheels! No, there's three. It's a tricycle, or what's left of one.* The front part had pulled away from the rest of the body, but, in her mind she could visualize how she could use this. *I'll attached this to those…ah…oh, yes, snowboards! And the boards to the trough and then to a…ah…oh I know, that wagon handle, and then I rig that up to the bike so I can tow it.*

It was easier said than done. It took Lacey a whole week of tinkering with her *contraption,* as she called it, to get it ready for a test ride. It towed quite easily behind the bike so she took it out with her for her morning ride. No problems! "Hey Winnie! I have good news. Lacey said when she got back to the cave. You're going for a ride." Winnie just kept chewing. But that didn't dampen Lacey's spirits. She put some blankets in the trough and pulled the goat over to it, picked her up and put her inside. Winnie only lasted about one-second, and then jumped right out. "Ah come on, it's all nice and cozy for you. Let's try that again." Two-seconds. Then it was a game of catch as Lacey chased the goat around the cave. Winnie ran down to the cave stream and jumped right in. "Sure, you'll jump in the water, but not in the…contraption…it's your…your…wagon, yes, yes, I'm calling it a wagon." Lacey went in after Winnie and they splashed around until she was able to get a noose over her neck and drag her out.

Every morning for the next few days, Lacey and Winnie would have the battle for the wagon. Finally, Lacey figured out a way to tie the goat in. Winnie kicked and kicked at the trough's sides denting them but they held. Lacey just let her go until she gave up and stood there bleating. Lacey then gave her a treat. The next morning, it was the same, and this time Winnie didn't kick as much. A week of this and Lacey figured it was time for a test ride.

Now she had to figure a way to cover the wagon so Winnie would be protected from the sun. Lacey took the extra coat and fashioned it to fit the trough. But she needed to make it like a roof. So she went back to the dig site to find something to make a frame for a roof. She found some old tent rods. *This is perfect.* She thought to herself. Back at home, she fashioned the roof frame and laid the coat over it. "Hey Winnie, it's time to try this out with the roof on it." Winnie came over, looking for a treat first. "Now just wait, you have to get in first." Lacey said as she lifted the goat in and secured her. But as Lacey put the roof on, Winnie jumped and bleated. The rope held her but she kicked so high that she got all tangled in the frame and coat. That made her even more scared and before Lacey knew it, the whole wagon was off the snowboards, on its side, twine unraveling, goat and roof all wound up together. It was…a disaster.

After getting the poor goat freed of the mess, Lacey just sat down and laughed. There was nothing else to do. "Well, I guess I will have to get you used to the roof now. And I don't know how long that will take. And I need something stronger than twine. I don't have enough rope" Winnie bleated loudly as she ran to her pen. The next morning Lacey was back at the dig site looking for anything stronger than twine. Then a few days later, she found a roll of wire. It was rusty, but strong enough. She brought it back to the cave and started the repairs. It took a few days to repair the damaged wagon and another two weeks past until Winnie was comfortable being in the wagon with the roof on. Lacey wheeled her around the cave at first just pulling her slowly to get used to that. Then she took Winnie out for a short ride. All seemed to go well with that. When she got back in the cave and opened the roof, Winnie was just standing there looking for a treat. She got two.

★　★　★

The ride down toward the valley was going smoothly. Winnie was doing okay and wasn't kicking or bleating too much. Lacey went past her usual turn to head back home as the morning light began to get brighter. This was it. No turning back. No matter what she felt, no matter what fear came into her mind she was determined to stay the course. She picked up speed. Then, a rattling noise made her slow down. The wheels on the cart were loosening. It was obvious that she wouldn't get as far as she hoped before the sun came up. But the further down into the valley she went the longer it would take for the full sun to hit her. She hoped that would compensate for how slow she was traveling. *I need to make it to the river crossing.* Lacey thought. She hunkered down and just kept riding.

The tingling on Lacey's back was getting more annoying now. She knew the bridge had to be close, but she didn't see any sign of the river crossing yet. She began looking around for some shelter in case she couldn't make it. It was getting harder and harder to concentrate as the familiar fears and thoughts were flooding in her mind. She kept shaking her head and trying to focus. Just when she thought she was going to lose it, Winnie started bleating, louder and louder. That was the distraction Lacey needed, so she began bleating along with Winnie. "Baa…baa." It was not a pleasant sound, but, it was what was needed. It was a symphony of bad noises. Wheels squeaking, bleats in and out of sync, the road noise from the bike wheels, and then, a noise of a river.

"There it is, Winnie! I can hear it. There it is, just down there. The river!" Lacey picked up speed again and could see around the bend a bridge. "There's the bridge, that's where we'll be safe."

The sun was almost at its high point as Lacey pulled off the road. She quickly gathered the provisions and stowed them under the bridge before coming back to get Winnie. They ran back under the bridge and hunkered down. She gave Winnie some water and drank some herself. She pulled Winnie close and put the coat from the wagon roof over them both and tried to rest. Winnie was restless at first but settled down. It was going to be a long day under this bridge.

★   ★   ★

Sleep was fitful as the fears seeped into Lacey's dreams. The voice in her dreams kept saying, 'Go back.' And the hallways kept closing in on her. She spoke up in her dream this time saying, "No. I am going on. I'm going on. I'm going!" But she felt glued to the floor. She could not move. The walls were getting tighter and she was so scared. In her dream she was trying so hard to move but felt paralyzed. Finally she could flinch a little and as the walls were squeezing her she freed her feet and woke up. She woke up in a sweat and screamed out. "Agh!" After a moment she settled down. Winnie was just staring at her, and then, gave her a nudge. "Okay, I'm okay. It's almost dusk. Let's eat and get on the road again."

Lacey took Winnie down to the river and they splashed around for a bit. The water was refreshing. Lacey checked her back, feeling for any lesions. Nothing felt too bad. She put some ointment on her back as best she could. Then she gave some food to Winnie and ate some of her dried tomatoes. She figured she could travel at least an hour in the dusk and maybe a bit more. But she really didn't know what was beyond this bridge. Her map just showed the lowlands with no specific roads or places. So from here on in, it would be true exploration. She would go as far as she could this evening and then in the early morning try to plot her progress on the map and draw a landmark on it so she could find her way back home. At least that was the plan.

The night ride went well and the two explorers made great progress. But as the morning approached the terrain changed. The road got thinner and thinner. Grass was overgrown and the pavement gave way to patchy grass and dirt. It slowed Lacey and Winnie way down. She began to look ahead for places of shade as the sunrise was approaching. There was a rocky crag that was to her west that could serve as a place to rest but it was up a steep hill. She kept going. The grass got thicker and it became harder to keep the cyclone moving. She tried stopping and revving up the flywheel, but then she would just spin in the grass. She just had to trudge along. Finally her speed was slower than if she walked.

Lacey looked around. The hills were quite a ways away. But there was the river. She had kept it in sight as she moved south. But there was no real shade. "Well, Winnie, we have no choice. We will be walking and maybe we can find a deep pool of water we can hide in. We're not giving up."

"Baa," was the reply. Lacey gathered up all she could carry and fashioned the protective coat over Winnie and they walked on. Now the sun was getting high in the sky so it was time to find shelter. Wading into the river was cool but there was no deep pool; and then, they came to some rapids. Lacey was really burning now and Winnie was agitated, obviously burning too. She had no choice but run to find a place to dig a hole. But, as Lacey turned to go to the bank, she slid off a rock and down she went into the water...the rapids sucking her in. She had hold of Winnies' rope and pulled her in with her. The poor goat let out a noise she had never heard. Lacey let go of the rope and lost sight of Winnie. Now the rapids got deeper and faster and Lacey was just trying to get to the bank. She was weighed down with all her gear and the protective coat was not helping. She gasped for air, got water in her lungs, and started coughing. She sank back under the water, pushed up from a rock, but hit her head on a larger boulder. She tried to push back up for air, but everything just went dark.

CHAPTER 2

Where Am I?

"LACEY! LACEY! CAN YOU HEAR ME? LACEY! CAN YOU HEAR ME? Lacey!" The voice seems so far away at first. Lacey can barely hear it, but then it gets closer and louder. Lacey opens her eyes and sees a face, but it's blurry, and her eyes are not steady. She tries to focus but she can't. She blinks and blinks but it is of no use. She tries to move but she is paralyzed. A voice says, "Lacey, everything is okay. You're all right. Just relax and remain calm." Lacey is trying to talk but nothing is coming out of her mouth. She's a bit scared but she is so relaxed that she remains calm.

"It will take a few moments before you gain your muscles. The sedative will wear off. So, just let it happen. I promise, you will be okay. If you can, move your feet and hands, that will help you."

Lacey suddenly realizes that she is not alone. There is another person in this world. This excites her and she has a million questions. But she can't speak. As the person moves away, all Lacey can see is a form. She still can't focus her eyes. *Who is this? Am I dreaming?* She wonders. The person comes near and says, "I'll be back in a little while. Don't worry, just keep moving your limbs and you will be able to see clearly in a bit." Then the person turns and leaves. Lacey is focused on moving. She remembers her last dream, a nightmare, really. And she is afraid it could become real if she can't move and

15

focus. It takes what seems like forever, but slowly she can see the wall, a clock hangs there. She has only seen pictures of clocks in her books. This one is real. She knows this because it's moving. She can hear the second hand clicking. *Where am I?* She wonders.

She moves her feet and hands faster and tries to raise her arm but realizes she is in a restraint. She fitfully moves her whole body now, but soon gets tired and stops. She focuses on the clock and listens to the ticking. This calms her and she just rests for a while. Then, the person comes back.

"Now, let's see if you can breathe on your own, shall we?" Lacey wonders what this means. I going to disconnect this tube and when I do, try to breathe, Okay?" Lacey feels the tube being disconnected and then sucks in some air.

"Very good! Now, we will get this tube out. Just breathe through your nose while I pull it out. This will be uncomfortable." Lacey feels the tube being ripped out. It seems like it takes a long time because the tube is so long, Lacey is gagging. But finally, she is free of the contraption and just says, "Yes!" Then she clears the frog from her throat and asks, "What was that? Who are you? Where am I? What's going on?"

"Rest now, the voice says, Just rest. There is plenty of time for questions"

Lacey says, "Please release my hands. I can't move."

"I will be back in the morning. You need your rest now." Then Lacey feels a prick and everything goes dark again.

Sunrise comes through the window and as Lacey tries to open her eyes, they stick and her lashes make the light wavy. She tries to free her eye lids; she wants to wipe her eyes, but she can't because her hands are still restrained. She just lays there. The light streaks are all colors and she plays with her lashes by closing her eyes all the way and then opening them as far as the gunk in her eyes will allow. What else can she do? She wonders when the person will return.

"Hello...Hello...Hello!" Lacey shouts out. But there is no reply. "I'm fine now, can I get up? Please get me out of these ropes." Again, no answer. Lacey takes a deep breath and tries to get her hands free but that just tires her out. Laying there, her lashes finally let go so she can look around the room. The clock is straight ahead, it's 8:25 in the morning. There are no pictures or anything else on the wall to her left. She can't see the wall behind her and the windows are to her right. The clouds outside are fluffy white and the sun is peeking through them as they move across the sky. Lacey watches them and then nods off.

"Lacey, Lacey." Her eyes open to see a face. But it's different from the one she saw before. "I am Ayla. I am taking care of you." Ayla releases the straps on Lacey's feet and hands. "Sit up now." Lacey feels the straps loosen and springs up. She gets dizzy and nearly falls over. "Slowly now, go slowly, Lacey." She steadies Lacey taking hold of her arm.

Lacey can see clearly that this Ayla is different. It's a person; or is it? Its form is sleek but bells outward at the bottom. It has a face and arms but it is not like Lacey.

Lacey gains her balance and looks at Ayla. "What are you?"

Ayla backs off. "What am I? I am Ayla; I take care of you."

"That didn't answer my question. You are not...like me. So what are you?"

"I am Ayla."

Lacey shakes her head. This form before her has a face, but everything about her body is smooth and light blue. It moves smoothly across the floor. The arms look right but the rest of the body is definitely a machine. "I know what you are! I've seen you in one of my books. You're a robot!"

"What is a robot?"

"You are. A robot is you."

"I am Ayla."

Lacy gets off the stretcher and walks around the room, tripping as she goes.

"Take care, Lacey, go slowly."

"How do you know my name?"

"I am Ayla, I take care of you." Ayla takes Lacey's arm as she walks.

"Is that all you can say?"

"I answered your question. Is there more I should say?"

"Never mind. You talk like me, but you are not like me." Lacy looks around the room. *There must be someone else here. The voice I heard before.* She thinks. The wall that was behind her stretcher has a door. Lacey heads for it, but Ayla cuts her off.

"That area is off limits."

"Why? What's in there?" Lacey tries to move around Ayla.

"That area is off limits."

Lacey raises her voice, "Hey! Someone! Help me! I need help! What is this place? Where am I?" Another prick. Darkness again.

★ ★ ★

The hallway is there. The voice is there. But Lacey can't move. The voice gets louder, "Lacey, Lacey!" Lacey jumps up out of her dream. It's dark. No one is in the room with her. She slides off the stretcher and moves toward the wall with the door. She is trying not to fall over but bumps into a table and knocks things off. She is sure the noise will bring Ayla. Lacey feels her way over to the door, hunkers down and waits. When Ayla opens it to come in, Lacey sees her chance. She pushes by the robot and runs into the hallway outside.

It's still dark. There are no windows. Lacey quickly moves down the hallway feeling the wall to guide her. There are no lights. She can hear Ayla moving toward her. She runs faster and faster until she runs into a wall. Sliding to the left she finds another hallway. *This is just like my dream, but no one is calling me.* She wonders about this when she hears Ayla from the other hallway. "Lacey, Lacey. Stop!" Lacey screams out, "Help! Help!" Lacey feels a door and goes through. Everything goes bright white. She covers her eyes, blinded by the light. It's the sun. She is outside.

Lacey looks around. She stands on a crag of a cliff. She looks down over the railing to see a sheer drop off of hundreds of feet. There is no where to go. The wind is strong and cold. She realizes she is only wearing light weight pants and top. The door has not opened so Ayla has not followed her through it. Seeing no other option, Lacey knocks but there is no answer. There is no handle to open it from outside. She looks to the sides and above the door, but there is nothing but rock. She sighs and says, "Phooey!" She sits down in a crevice bringing her knees to her chest and wrapping her arms around her legs. Looking down at her bare feet she knows she can't last long out here in the freezing cold, and of course, the sun is right there glaring at her. She suddenly remembers, "Winnie!" She gets up and bangs on the door harder. She yells for help over and over. Her hands are getting raw now and her feet are numb. Just when she's about to give up…the door opens, she is pulled inside and she feels a prick…darkness.

★   ★   ★

Lacey opens her eyes and sees, not Ayla, but a person like herself. A woman with long white hair and deep brown eyes. Her hair is pulled back into a pony tail and she is dressed all in white. "Lacey! Hello. I am Dr. Zahn." Lacey notices her voice is different from her own and the robots. "You gave us quite a scare there. We weren't sure where you went. You could have fallen and, well, I am glad you didn't. Ayla was frantic."

"Where is Winnie?"

"Who?"

"My goat! Where is she? I lost her in the river."

"So you named your goat, that's very good."

"Yes, of course, why wouldn't I? Hey! Where am I? What is this place and why am I here…and why are we on the side of a mountain? What is going on? Why do you keep sticking me with a needle?"

"Okay, slow down. I will tell you everything you need to know. But as to your first question…Winnie, your goat. Well, you need not worry about her. She will be fine, it's just part of the program."

Lacey sits up, "Program? What program? What does that mean? Where is Winnie?"

"Just relax, you need to get acclimated to your new surroundings here. There'll be plenty of time to tell you about Winnie and everything else that is part of the program, which, by the way, you have excelled in."

Lacey just shakes her head. This is all so confusing. She bends her knees up to her chest and rocks her body. Dr. Zahn puts her arm around Lacey and says, "It will be okay. Just try to remain calm."

"Remain calm? I don't know what's happening, I don't know exactly where I am, or why; and I thought I was the only person in this country, or at least where my home is. And...why do you talk funny?

"Funny? Oh, for you, I have what is called an accent. It is because my parents were from Germany. This, country, being Scotland, I gave you a Scottish accent. My parents were Jewish, Ashkenazi to be exact...which is...well, it's a long story...but for now...yes, I talk different from the way you do."

"I have no idea what all that means."

"Don't worry about it. So, what do you remember?"

"It has been just Winnie and me since I can remember." Lacey thinks for a moment. "I really don't remember much before I found myself in my home last fall. How come I can't remember anything? I know my name and I know how to do stuff. But I can't remember... parents or family or anything." Then Lacey looks straight at the doctor, stands up and gets right in her face. "Who are you? What are you doing to me? Where am I?"

The doctor backs up and Ayla zooms in between them. "Please remain calm." She says.

"Ayla, where have you been? I thought you would follow me out that door."

"I am here to help you, but not help you to hurt yourself."

"Or the doctor, I can see."

"Yes, please don't hurt my maker."

"Your maker?"

Dr. Zahn steps in between them and says, "That's okay Ayla, I'm fine. Please go back to your spot." Ayla moves back to a red dot and stops beside it. "Ayla can only move to certain designated spots. That's why she could not follow you all the way down the corridor. You may have imagined her chasing you, but she could not. There are no designated spots that way. We lost power, and the lights were out for a few minutes. I'm sorry you got scared and ran. But please understand, we are not going to hurt you."

"Well, then help me. Help me find Winnie and get me back…" Lacey stopped short. She remembers the vow she made to let nothing make her turn back toward home.

"Don't worry, you will be back with Winnie shortly."

Then, that damned prick. Darkness once more.

CHAPTER 3

Finding the Source

LACEY WOKE UP ON THE RIVER BANK. SOMEONE WAS LICKING HER face. She opened her eyes to see Winnie. "Oh Winnie! You're all right!" Lacey gave her a hug. Winnie, whinnied…not her usual bleat. It seemed Winnie was glad to see Lacey too. Lacy let go of the goat, got up and looked around. "Wait…wait…aah how did I get here? I was just in a room with the doctor and that robot. What is going on?" "Baa." Was the only reply.

"I've got to find that mountain. I need to get back in there and find that doctor." But then, Lacey remembered she'd lost all her provisions. The bike, the food and her protective coat. Panic began to set in as she looked up to a full sun coming over the horizon and her coat was gone. All she had on was her linens.

"We've got to find shelter."

"Baa." Winnie was eating grass.

"I'm so hungry. What am I going to eat?" Lacey saw that Winnie's udder was full. So she cupped one hand to catch some milk as she pulled down on Winnie's teat with the other. Winnie was used to this so she just kept on eating. The milk tasted so good. But it wouldn't be enough. Lacey needed to find something substantial to eat. She looked around and then noticed flowers…they were everywhere. Shades of purple and pink, white and yellow. And the sun, it was getting high in the sky, but she wasn't feeling any burning. "Something is very different…this is wrong."

Lacey remembered hitting her head. She felt her scalp but there was no cut or scab or tenderness. She saw some clover, picked it and ate. She spied some little wild berries. "Not sure what this is but I'm eating it, if you are, Winnie." After filling her belly enough, Lacey started exploring. She was not in the highlands anymore. There were more trees and a small loch nearby. As she went over to the shore line she looked around and saw tall buildings in the distance. Then she looked at her reflection in the water. "Well, it's me… that's something…and you are still you. But where are we?" Winnie was drawn away by a low hanging fir branch. Lacey followed and then she spied a building. It wasn't far away. She didn't know what it was, but it was a shelter so she tried to coax Winnie to follow her. The rope was long gone, so she had to entice the goat with a nice branch off a pine tree. Winnie was loving the pine needles. "Come, Winnie, this is your new food. You like it don't you?" She followed slowly, being distracted a few times by the tasty grass and flowers. As they walked along, Lacey just shook her head… *This is just not right.*

Finally, entering the building at dusk, Lacey saw that it was a station of some sort. There were no tracks outside but it looked like rail stations she'd seen in books. There was no one there. She wandered around and saw two doors. Each door had a figure of a man and a woman on them. She went through the men's door and saw something she never had before. There were glass mirrors and basins. There were smaller doors on stalls with large bowls on the floor with lids. She went in one and pulled up the lid and there it was. "That's the weird yoke I saw at the hollow! Hey Winnie! Come here." Winnie followed her in and went to the bowl for a drink. Lacey moved over to the next one and saw what looked like ancient mud in it. The smell was suffocating. "Winnie! Don't drink that water…this…this…I know what this is! This is where you leave your waste. You definitely don't eat or drink in here. Come on."

Lacey left there and looked around. The walls had large frames of shiny black glass. No pictures, just a blank black shiny board. *That's weird,* She thought. Then she saw some stairs and went down cautiously to find a large long room with a large tube opening. Again she saw the same blank black boards, only smaller. There was a door…she tried to open it but it was locked. "What does this door lead to? I need to find something to open it. Come on Winnie let's go back up and see what we can find." Winnie seemed to understand every word Lacey said. And she seemed closer than she ever was before. Lacey liked that and kept petting her as she searched around. She found a closet with tools and a few things she thought she could use to open the door.

Getting the door open took some time but she finally got in. It was very dark and she couldn't see much so she felt around and found a lever. It was pointed down and so she pushed up on it. Instantly there was light everywhere in the room and the building. The boards suddenly flickered and came to life. They had colored lines and destinations. *This is definitely a train station. But where are the trains?* She wondered. Just then the tube was making noise and a whooshing tubular car rushed in the room and stopped. "Winnie! Did you see that? What is it? It certainly doesn't look like any train car I've seen in my books. And where are the tracks?" As usual Winnies reply was, "Baa." The doors opened to the car. Lacey stuck her head inside and looked wearily at the seats. Winnie just walked right in and started heading to the front of the car. "Winnie! Don't just walk in places you don't know about." But she was already chewing on a seat. Lacey followed her in.

"Don't eat that seat! Bad Winnie."

"Baa."

"Not baa, bad."

Just then the door shut and an announcement came over a speaker. "Please take your seat or hold on to the railing above you. We are leaving the station now." Lacey was jolted into a seat next to Winnie and off they went into the tunnel. She felt the speed as she was pushed back into the seat. "We're moving pretty fast. I just wonder where we're headed and where we are. This is crazy."

★   ★   ★

It seemed Lacey and Winnie came to a stop just a few minutes after they left the station. The doors opened again to another long dark room. Lacey had kept her tools in her hand. So she knew what to do. Opening this door took longer but she got in and pushed that lever up. "We have lights. Now let's find out where we are." Trotting up the stairs she could see that this was a much larger station with grand ceilings and huge windows. Lacey saw taller buildings outside. "This is a city...it's what I saw back at the station. But again, where are the people?" A large board said, "Welcome to Glasgow." "So that's where we are. But where is the doctor? That lab or whatever it was in that mountain, is not here in this city, that's for sure." Lacey found a bench and sat down. Winnie came by and sat at her feet.

"What's with you Winnie? You are never this affectionate. You're becoming like those dogs I read about."

"Baa."

"It's been a long day and I'm tired. Let's get some rest."

At that they settled in on that bench for the night, Lacey drifted off to sleep in her thoughts. *I should go exploring while it's dark, but I'm just too tired. Besides, we should take that tube back north and see if we can get to the highlands and that mountain.*

★   ★   ★

"Lacey!" It was the same dream. Lacey woke up to the morning sun plowing through the large windows of the station. The rays were full of dust particles and Lacey noticed there wasn't any irritation on her skin. Winnie was scrounging paper cups and whatever she could find to chew on. "Winnie! Don't eat that!" Winnie just looked at Lacey and chewed on. "Come on, let's go outside and see what's out there in this... Glasgow." Winnie was not following so Lacey found a rope on a stand and fashioned a lead. She had to really pull hard

25

to get Winnie out the door, but once they were outside Winnie was pulling Lacey down the street.

"Hey, wait."

"Baa."

Winnie was on to some smell or something and just kept pulling Lacey down the street. It was a pine tree in a median. The goat happily ate at the branches while Lacey looked around. She saw a large building; its sign said, "R.O.P. Services" and there was a door under it. "Let's go over there." Lacey said. But the goat was not interested, so Lacy tied her off to the base of the pine tree and went over to inspect. The door was locked and barred off. Her tools would not get her in this time. She turned away and wondered what R.O.P stood for.

Seeing Winnie was still occupied, Lacey walked further and saw posters pasted on the walls of buildings. They said, "Find the Source," whatever that meant. *This is crazy. What does all this mean?* She wondered. Walking on, she saw other hand written sayings on walls. "Who is the creator now?" And "Only clean blood allowed" Then a sign with someone's picture and across the photo the word, 'Source' stamped in red. And there were skulls and other words she had never seen in her books back at the cave. It was all too disturbing. She turned back toward Winnie.

"Let's go back to the station and see if we can get a ride north." Lacey untied Winnie and pulled her away from the tree. Back in the station she looked around for some kind of office or directory to the routes. The boards were not working even though the lights were on. She didn't want to just go in the tube without knowing which direction it would take them. She found an office and rifled through the papers that were all over the floors and desks. There was nothing helpful.

Lacey came out of the office area. "I can't believe there are no directories here. How is that possible? How can you run a tube train without a schedule?" Winnie was chewing on something and just looked up without even a little bleat. Lacey sat down in frustration near the windows and yelled out, "I need to get back to the highlands...to that mountain! To Dr...aah...Dr. Zahn!" She sighed and just stared out the window.

But within a few minutes, a car pulled up to the door and announced, "Ride share to Ben Macdui is waiting." Lacey looked around, even though she had not seen another person. "Are you kidding me?" The car announced the destination again. "Winnie, I think we found a ride. Let's go!"

She pulled the goat to the car and they got in.

"Who is Ben Macdui? I asked for Dr. Zahn."

The car replied, "Ben Macdui is a mountain; it is where Dr. Zahn is."

"All I had to do was ask for the doctor?"

"Our services include finding anyone, anywhere in the country and taking you to them. We hope you are comfortable for the long ride ahead. The last leg will be a flight in our Heli-Taxi."

Lacey sat back as they drove out of the city. There was no other traffic. She finally asked, "Umm...where are all the other cars? Where is everyone?"

The car answered, "I am a transport. I have no other information than your destination."

"So you're a robot?"

"I am a transport."

"Oh not this again, just like Ayla."

"I have no location information for an Ayla."

"Never mind. Just get us to that flying taxi."

"Another hour to the Heli-Taxi."

"Is there any food around here?"

"Complimentary snacks are in the center console. Please help yourself and enjoy."

Lacey opened the console and found boxes with colors and the words Cookies and Fruit. She had never seen these before. "Look, Winnie, food in a box."

"The car said, "Dried Apricots and cookies. Enjoy!"

Lacey opened a box and found the dried fruit inside a foil wrapper. "I have never had any fruit before. And I have never heard of these...

but…well, we'll see." Lacey took a bite. "Sweet! I like them." She gave one to Winnie, who then tried to take the whole wrapper. Lacey pulled it away, but Winnie jumped on Lacey and grabbed the wrapper in her mouth, and the whole thing ripped open and fruit went everywhere. "Bad goat! It's a good thing there is more of these."

Settling down for the ride they snacked away. The cookies were quite stale, but still filling. "These are no better than my bread back at the cave."

"Baa"

"Hey! I didn't ask for your opinion."

★　★　★

After eating, it wasn't long before Lacey fell asleep. She awoke to a loud beeping sound, and the transport voice saying, "Please exit the vehicle. The door will close in one minute. Once closed it will not open again until I reach the next destination." Lacey cleared her eyes and looked around. Winnie was gone. Lacey jumped out as the door was closing on her, but reached back in quick to grab a few more snack boxes. Then she looked around for Winnie as the transport left. She could see a large object she figured was this heli-taxi. It had an oval body and four large circular, what looked like windmill blades like she'd seen in her books, just a lot smaller. There was a bright red line painted on the pavement. She kept calling out for Winnie, but there was no answer. She stepped over the red line, and as soon as she did, there was another loud beeping sound followed by an announcement. "Please enter the transport now. The door will close in five minutes. Store your bags in the open cargo bay. The weight is calculated for safe flight. If your bags are too heavy the transport will not take off until you lighten the load."

"Well, no worries there, it's just me, this food and my goat. That is if I can find her. Five minutes…I will be right back. Don't take off without me."

Now frantic, Lacey ran around looking for Winnie. She couldn't see her anywhere. Lacey screamed over and over…"WINNIE!!" But there was not a sound. Lacey had tears in her eyes as she screamed out once more, "I can't lose you again! Winnie!" As she slowly turned back toward the heli-taxi, Winnie came out of a building opening with a large garbage bag in her teeth. She had ripped it open and all kinds of dirty and old garbage was falling out as she merrily trotted along. Lacey looked at her and just shook her head and let out a relieved but exasperated laugh. "Winnie! Come on, we've got to go!" She ran and grabbed the rope, which was amazingly still attached to the goat. They got in the heli-taxi as the door was just beginning to close. The garbage bag was dragged in with them. Winnie was not about to let go of her treasure.

It was another first for Lacey, and Winnie. She had never been in a train or car much less fly in a heli-taxi. "I will now take you to the landing area at R.O.P. Labs. Please sit back, buckle in and put on the ear buds in the console in front of you. This flight will take about ten minutes." The sound of the windmill blades was loud and then the ground just fell away. Lacey was glued to the window looking down on the great expanse below. Winnie was only interested in one thing…her garbage…which reeked. But Lacey didn't care…she was holding her nose looking out at the mountain side, mesmerized by it all. As the heli-taxi rose above the clouds, Lacey remembered the sign on the building back in Glasgow.

"R.O.P. Services…I saw that in the city. So we are going to them? Is that where Dr. Zahn is? It must be. It's all the same company right?"

"The R.O.P. Lab is on Ben Macdui. R.O.P. Services building is in Glasgow. I can turn back if you so desire."

"No! No…just stay on your course…and…thank you."

"It is our pleasure to provide you the quickest and safest transport."

Lacey thought a moment and asked, "How many times have you made this trip up the mountain?"

"I am not authorized to share that information."

"Ok…but when was the last time you made this trip."

"I am not able to access the flight time log."

"Yeah, okay. It was the same with that…what did it call itself?… Ride Share. No answers. You robots aren't very informative, are you?"

Winnie agreed, "Baa."

Just then the heli-taxi dropped straight down about a hundred meters. Lacey screamed as Winnie was floating up to the ceiling. Lacey grabbed her rope and pulled her back down in an instant. They rose back up as the voice said, "Just a little turbulence. Nothing to worry ab-ba-ba-bout. Make sure your seeee-belts are f-fastened."

"Turbulence?! That scared me to death! Why are you speaking so weird?"

"The landing site … up the cliff. We…landing sh-shortly." Now, the voice was cutting in and out. Lacey could not see a landing area. The heli-taxi began rocking and moving from side to side quite violently. And then, CRASH!

CHAPTER 4

What Am I?

LACEY AWAKES IN THE SAME HOSPITAL ROOM WITH THE SAME TUBE down her throat with Ayla looking over her. Strapped in as before, and of course she can't move. This is getting to be old. Ayla moves back and calls Dr. Zahn on the intercom. Lacey's eyes are again messed up. She can't seem to focus and see the clock clearly. She has so many questions and is really confused. Dr. Zahn comes in and says, "Hi there, Lacey. Do you remember me?" Lacey shakes her head yes, but is glaring at the doctor.

"I can see you are confused, maybe even angry. That's okay, it's to be expected seeing all you have been through in the program. Just give me a few minutes to check your vitals and then I will remove the tube so you can talk."

Program? What is that? Get this tube out of me...please. Lacey can think it...but she can't say it. But when the tube is out, then Lacey yells at the doctor.

"What is going on? Why am I here? What happened? I was just on a heli-taxi and...and...it CRASHED! Where is Winnie?!"

"Just try to breathe deeply. It will help calm you."

"I don't want to be calm. I want answers!"

"You are all right. The crash wasn't...well...not really real."

"Not real? What?!"

31

"It's the program. We call it the IBS which stands for In Body Simulation. You're connected to a…well…have you read in any of your books at your home about computers?"

"Computers? What are they?"

"Okay, so…uhm…it's hard to explain, but you are connected to this computer that runs the In Body Simulation or Sim for short. It places you in varied environments for different tests. To see how you get along. To give you…to have you…experience different things to help you grow in your understanding of this world."

"I'm connected to a computer…how?"

"There is a…what we call a chip in the back of your neck."

"Is that the prick I feel?"

"Prick? Well, I suppose it could present that way."

"Present that way? What are you talking about? It is an annoying prick and every time I feel it everything goes dark and then I wake up…well, sometimes here…but not always here…I wake up outside. Where is Winnie?"

"Okay. Enough questions for today. You need your rest and tomorrow we can get you up and walking and then I will explain everything." Dr. Zahn looks at Ayla who nods and moves her hand to press a key on the computer keyboard.

Lacey figures out what this means. "No, wait!" Prick…darkness.

Ayla taps Lacey. She opens her eyes and can see. "I want Dr. Zahn! NOW!" "Good morning, Lacey, the doctor will be in shortly, but let's get you up and walking shall we?" Ayla's calm manner quells Lacey's anxiety a bit, but she is determined to get answers. Lacey looks again at Ayla and notices how she moves from dot to dot, smoothly skimming across the floor. When she has to turn, her head turns first and her body follows. Her head and arms look human and move like she is human, but clearly, she is not.

Lacey tries a different tact. "So, Ayla, how long have you been here?"

"I don't have that information."

"Of course you don't. I haven't met one of you…whatever you are, that has any answers"

"Please take a few steps around the room so you can get acclimated to walking again."

"Again? What does that mean? I can walk. I have been…I always have."

"Please take a few steps. Remember last time you tripped at first."

"I only remember running out the door into the freezing air."

Dr. Zahn walks in and says, "Good morning."

"Answers, Dr. Zahn. I want answers. And no more pricks!"

"No more pricks. I promise. Now let's go into my office. It's much more comfortable there. Come, take my arm."

Lacey feels strangely comfortable walking beside the doctor. Arm in arm seems a natural thing and the warmth of another humans touch is a new experience. It's nice. The office has two chairs facing each other and as soon as Lacey sits down she asks, "What is Ayla? A robot or what?"

"You could call her that I suppose, but I prefer to think of her as just…a care giver. And she is a good one at that."

"How come she can't answer my questions?"

"Well, that depends on what you ask."

"She doesn't know how long she's been here. That's pretty basic information isn't it?"

"Okay…so…there was a decision a long time ago that all sentient entities be limited in the information they could access. You see, about two hundred years ago when artificial intelligence, or AI, as they called it, was beginning to spread into all of life, there were attempts at letting these self-learning computer programs or AI, be used in robots and many other applications."

"So is Ayla an…AI?"

"Well, yes, but she is limited."

"Why?"

"Like I said, way back they tried to let AI run…free, I guess you could say…but it did not go well. You see, without a…conscience or soul…or you could say, without human experience in real time… it just failed. Messed up things pretty badly. So then, the unlimited self-learning AI's were only programed into computers. They are not allowed in mobile devices like Ayla."

"That's why the car and heli-taxi couldn't give me any information."

"Yes. Their parameters are very limited to their immediate function."

"Why did it crash? And, for the last time…Where is Winnie?"

Dr. Zahn gave out a long sigh. "Well, first let me say that what you experienced in the heli-taxi was not real, really."

"Not real?! What do you mean, not real? It was…so real."

"Yes, for you it was, and…is…but isn't."

"What?"

"Let me explain. But I need to go back to the past to fully explain. Please listen and be patient…we will get to all your questions…even about your goat."

"Winnie."

"Yes, Winnie. Now let's start at the beginning…or I should say… the ending. I'm going to tell you it all very fast and I ask you to wait to ask any questions. It is a dark part of human history and I am not proud of it. But here goes. You see, two hundred years ago, there was this group of scientists who wanted to see if they could continue efforts to sterilize what they called, "Inferior races," as had been tried before, in what we call, the mid–twentieth century. It was at first meant to sterilized only one race, but it mutated and affected all races.

By the time the world understood…it was too late. No more babies. That caused a global market for children under the age of five. Abductions, auctions…so many parents were killed for their kids. Civil society broke down. Nations vied for young ones to continue their national interests until a vaccine could be developed. Tactical nuclear war broke out in just about every country. The richest and most powerful took all they could and waited for the fall out to stop.

But before all that, there was the sterilization. The planning for this…this mass sterilization took a decade. There were millions of

34

mini-drones produced along with the virus which had been developed decades before. When the drones, which flew like bees, were released they sprayed the virus on strategic places, all it needed was an open pore in the skin. They sprayed among the populations that were intended to be sterilized. But there were unforeseen consequences. The spray mechanism didn't always work. The winds took the drones off course. It really was a bad distribution method. Animals caught it. It mutated. It affected every race. And the drones had a battery life of six weeks. When they dropped from the sky, they were thrown away or left on the streets, rivers and fields. They leached any leftover virus and their battery chemicals into the waste systems. So, the virus and toxic chemicals, eventually went everywhere.

The only safe places were in high elevations in very cool climates. The least popular places to live were the safest. But they were also the least populated. Eventually, natural deaths exceeded births, even with folks who were not touched by the virus or the wars. Anyone who was deemed able to bare a child was hunted down, but as soon as they were taken to a breeding facility, the virus inevitably got to them or their offspring. Many never got to a facility with all the factions and governments vying for them. It was mayhem at its worst. Now, this all happened over the last one hundred and fifty years. It is hard to process how it was not recognized for what it became. No one seemed to see it. But here we are.

Also, there were these…seed banks…sperm banks…egg banks… these are what make babies. They were taken over by the most powerful. The war over them was disastrous…all of them were destroyed. There was this age old, 'If I can't have it, no one can' mentality, and it ruled the day. And all DNA research facilities were destroyed in the fighting except for one. The PFHS, Preservation For Human Survival facility. It was run by a secret society of people who understood the threat these sterilization viruses posed. Decades ago they began secretly preserving DNA strands. They stole them from their work place, and donated their own. They donated eggs and sperms. Their supply was limited but they had good facilities and they had an ace coder, who began creating a program called RePop.

Given the directive to repopulate the earth if needed. Climate change or an extinction event prompted them to begin the work. But what happened to the world was not in their imaginations. No one paid too much attention to them because the thought of an extinction event was so remote in peoples minds. Oh there were plenty of warnings but the powerful didn't seem to believe it would really happen. But this secret society was able to secure land in the highlands of Scotland and build facilities there, and a secret one in the side of a mountain. They lived there for many years but so many were already sterile, having offspring was not easy. But using the eggs and sperm they had they were able to continue a small community, until death overcame their own births. But a few went into the secret lab, all inside the mountain. This very mountain, the one that we are in."

Lacey just sits there...shaking her head, and then asks, "What has this all got to do with me and Winnie?"

"That is an interesting story. So, I...I am...the last human. And it was bound to happen, the way the world outside went. We destroyed ourselves all while trying to hold on to our lives. The selfishness of the self, killed all the selves. But, I survived, hidden here with my work in this self sustaining environment. I have not been outside in many years. Even though we are high enough in altitude, I guess I have a fear of getting sick from anything, seeing as how I am alone...I am the last human...if I die, this work will end and that will be the end of the human race."

"Wait...wait...wait! You said, if *you* die...you are the last human... you? So...then, what am I?"

"Well, you...you are...a test."

"A test? What does that mean?"

"You...are...how shall I say it...human-esque? Kinda, almost human?"

Lacey is feeling her body, arms, legs, head, hair, face... "What are you talking about?" I have seen myself in the mirror. I am as human as you. I look like you. I'm not like Ayla. What do you mean?"

"Yes, you have a body, but it is...not completely...this is going to be hard to hear, so please listen. Your body, it looks right on the outside but inside…it has enhancements…bionics. So, to be honest, you are partly mechanical and partly biological."

Now Lacey is scared and jumps up out of the chair. "I don't believe you! You're lying!" She paces the room and then crouches down looking at her toes. "If these are not real…show me!"

"Come with me."

Lacey follows Dr. Zahn back to the room where she woke up.

"Here, place your foot on this pad." Lacey sits on a bench and places her foot where the doctor instructs.

"This is an x-ray…it can show you what is inside." Dr. Zahn shows Lacey a print of a normal foot. "Now look at that screen on the wall there." Doctor Zahn puts the x-ray over Lacey's foot and covers her lower body with a heavy sheet.

"That feels like my protective coat."

"Yes, It would."

"Hey, I have seen this…in one of my books…it looks through the your skin right to your bones."

"Okay, so you know. Now look at the screen."

The screen shows what is clearly a manufactured bone structure. Lacey's face goes blank. She then lays back on the bench, turns on her side and curls up in a ball. Dr. Zahn looks at Ayla who removes the protective sheet and then replaces it with a blanket.

"Why don't you rest for a while. I know this is a lot to take in."

Lacey doesn't answer.

"Rest now." Ayla says as she caresses Lacey's back.

Dr. Zahn moves to the door and says, "We'll talk more later. Just rest…and you won't feel a prick this time."

★ ★ ★

Lacey finds herself in a dreamworld. Colors are moving through the air like luminescent flowers floating all around her. They fade in and out. She too, is floating. Her hand moves in front of her and she can see right through it. She calls out for Winnie, but there is no answer. She tries to move forward but she is not standing on anything. She is just wiggling around but she can't get anywhere. Suddenly everything is spinning faster and faster and getting sucked down into a vortex. She tries to move away but she can't and just as she is getting sucked down…she wakes up.

"Aaah!"

"Are you okay?" Ayla asks.

"NO! No! I am not okay and I don't want to talk about it." *What a terrible dream,* She thinks it but doesn't say it.

"Here, let me give you a neck massage. That will make you feel better." Before Lacey can object, Ayla is behind her and gently massaging her neck and shoulders. This is a new experience for Lacey, and it feels so good, she just goes with it.

"There, there; just relax and tell me all about it."

Lacey turns and looks at Ayla, "Do you know that you are not human?"

"I am a care giver."

"So you really don't know what you are?"

"I am…"

"I know, A CARE GIVER!" Lacey grabs hold of Ayla and begins to cry. She has never done that. It is unsettling, but also it feels good. She pushes away and shakes her head. Ayla immediately gets her a tissue. Lacey composes herself. "I'm sorry, it's just so frustrating trying to figure out what is going on here. I just found out that I am not…well not what I thought I was. I'm not real. I'm, what did she say? A test? What is that?"

"You are humanity's last hope. That is what Dr. Zahn says."

"You heard her say that? But I'm not human, or I am…almost. I don't get it. Why am I like this? Don't you wonder why you are what you are?"

"I know what I am. I always have."

"Always? How long have you been here? Never mind, I know you don't have access to that information."

Just then Dr. Zahn walks in. "One hundred years. Ayla has been here longer than I have. She was my care giver when I was young."

"And how long have you been here?"

"Well, all my life; but if you're asking how old I am, I am eighty this year."

"How old am I…or should I ask, what is my turn on date."

"Oh, my dear Lacey, Don't despair, I know this is a hard thing to understand and take in. But I promise this will get better. You are so amazing. Your resilience and imagination, your natural engineering abilities, and your empathy are so beautiful to witness. I believe you are ready to move on to the next phase of your training."

Just then Lacey remembers Winnie. "Hey, what about Winnie? You said you would tell me about her."

"Yes, well, do you think you are ready to hear more?"

"Why not? What can be worse than finding out I am not really real."

"You are real. You are yourself. You know that. It's just that your body is not, well…" Dr. Zahn turns to get a tablet, but as she does she murmurs, "But I understand how you're feeling, it's kinda like finding out you are the last human."

Lacey looks at her for a moment and then touches her shoulder. "Wow! How old were you when…whoever told you? That must have been like crashing into the side of a mountain."

Dr. Zahn gives out a short laugh and looks at Lacey. "You really are growing so wonderfully, I like your sense of humor."

"Growing?"

"It's an expression. It means you are maturing in your mental capacity for empathy, sympathy and humor. You see without those three human traits there can be no civilization. And when those traits get clouded over with greed and survival instincts…well, this is how we ended up here."

"I am not feeling very mature. I…I don't know. I feel angry and scared. I feel…"

"Lost?"

"Yes! That's it. I feel lost. I don't know who I am. I don't understand why I am…"

"Here in this place and in the Sims?"

"Yes, please tell me everything. And please, please tell me about Winnie!"

"Okay, let's go back to my office."

★ ★ ★

As they sit down Dr. Zahn tells Lacey about how she designed Winnie. "There are what we call clones. These are animals that are basically copies of other animals with all the same genetic traits. Winnie is a clone. When she...well...expires...I replace her with another."

"What? Expire? That means she died, right?"

"Yes."

"Wait, so, she drowned in the river?"

"That's right."

"But then she was back."

"That was another clone."

"No...it can't be. She knew me."

"Yes, she has the same type of chip you do. So the experiences carry over from one Sim to the next."

Lacey looks around, shakes her head and says, "Where is she now?"

"Well...do you want to meet her? She is Winnie number three."

"Yes! Of course. And she has the memories. She will know me, right?"

"Yes, she will."

They go down a hallway and through a door. The smell reminds Lacey of her cave home. In fact, as she looks around she can see that is exactly what this is. There are animals all around and pens for them.

"We have some livestock. Not anywhere close to what used to be, but we hope one day they will come back. There are some in the wild, but we don't know if they will survive. But, we have all the DNA strands."

"What does that mean?"

"That's for another time, but first, here is Winnie."

Lacey turns and sees the goat in a pen. She rushes in and slides down at the goat's face and gives her a hug. Winnie number three

40

responds with a bleat and a head butt. Lacey frolics around for a bit, but then moves over to the wall and sits alone.

"What are you thinking?"

"It's hard to think that this Winnie is not…I don't know. Wait! Am I a clone? Would you let a cloned human die?

"You are not a clone. We would never produce human clones for experimentation."

"But why did the others goats have to die? What kind of test is that?" Why am I here? And why did Ayla say I was humanity's last hope? And another thing, Ayla called you her maker. But she is older than you."

"Maker is a generic term for the team. I didn't design or build Ayla, but I maintain her and so I am a part of the team that manufactured her, so I am her maker. Now as to the other thing she said, she should not have laid that on you. But it's not her fault. I should have never told her that."

"But you did. What did you mean by me being humanity's last hope, when I am not even human?"

Dr. Zahn sits down next to Lacey. "I am the last…the last. And I have lived with that knowledge for a long time. I have had to be extra careful about everything I do, so that I can live as long as possible to…well…start the human race over again. And you, my dear are my attempt to do just that. I have worked many years on your program."

"My program…the Sims? How many have I been through?" Just then, Winnie comes over and Lacey pets her. "Wait! If Winnie died, then so did I…I died in that crash! And even if I am not a clone…I died, right?"

"Well, yes, and no…not exactly…your body is…well…manufactured."

"Manufactured? What does that mean?"

"Well, you know you have a special bone structure. Your muscles, your skin and some, organs are grown here…it's very complicated. We have an AI that can basically print your body muscles and skin over the organs and the composite skeleton along with the fiber optic nerve system. It all connects to your brain chip."

Lacey is staring blankly again.

"But Lacey, listen to me; you, the essence of you did not die. It is housed in the skeletal part of your head. It remains, in sleep mode until the new body is reprinted again."

"So, when I hit my head on that rock in the river...I..."

"Drowned. Yes, and when the heli-taxi crashed, you died. But again, you didn't...just the body you inhabited. Thats why the Sim is called In Body Simulation. You're essence is downloaded into a... well...disposable body."

"Disposable?"

"I'm sorry, that's a bad term. But, we had no choice but to come up with a way to test you out without killing you. Animals can be cloned."

"So Winnie is number three...how many am I?"

"Well, it took a long time to develop your body. And there were failures...but this last generation of bodies worked, and the one you were in when you were in the cave was the first one to successfully have flesh co-exist with...well, we say metal for short, even though it's really a fiber alloy. But I'm getting on a tangent. So, to get back to your question, yes, you could say you are Lacey in body number three."

"So, is the world outside this mountain as empty as I remember? And why wasn't the sun as bad in the city? How did I get in my cave? What is real and what is the Sim?"

"Okay, so the world outside is pretty bad. It is real, it's not like they used to say, virtual. It is real for your body and for you, but, when your body dies, `well, as they used to say many hundreds of years ago...you get a redo."

"Redo? What does that mean?"

"Umm...let me show you. Follow me back to my office."

Lacey gets up to follow and Winnie comes follows her to the door.

"Can Winnie come too?"

"Sure."

Dr. Zahn goes into her office and sits on a lower longer chair. It is very fluffy.

"Come sit by me on the couch." Lacey sits down and sinks in. "That feels…nice."

"One of the few comfortable places to sit around here. Now look at the screen."

Dr. Zahn picks up a controller and a game comes on the screen. The beeps and funny characters take Lacey aback.

"This looks like some of my books, but the characters don't move."

"I want to show you this. It's called a video game. It is hundreds of years old. It's called Super Mario 3. Now watch. I kinda become Mario on a quest. And as Mario, I have three lives. So if I die, I have two more. And if I should lose those two, I can always start over."

"So, I am like this Mario?"

"Yes, but for real, it is no game we are engaged in. This is the last chance for humanity to begin again. If this fails…there are no redos."

Lacey sits back and takes a deep sigh.

Dr. Zahn puts the game away and sits back down. "Now as for the city, you asked me why the sun wasn't so bad there. That's because it has a dome over the city and outlying areas. I'll show you pictures. As for how you got to your cave home, we have a transport that is capable of transporting you and Winnie to where ever the Sim starts or is interrupted. It took you to the cave home. We gave you enough knowledge to live and survive. But everything else you experience was your own learning and your own innovation. That is the goal for the Sim"

"Now, I remember being scared to go too far from my home. Was that the…IB…S?"

"Yes, the In Body Simulation. The fear was a safety protocol built in to your program. But you broke through that, which was one of my goals for you."

"But that led me to drowning."

"Yes, but you got a redo. In this body, this manufactured body, you can live, but your mind and essence are backed up here, and experienced out there, by the chip. It stays connected to you at all times while you're in the Sim. Even as you drowned you were backed up here."

"So is my, essence in this body? Now? Or am I in some computer?"

"Yes, both are true. You are in your body, and you are backed up here. Actually, in the next room over."

"The next room over? I Don't understand."

"It's okay. This will take some time, and just so you know, that room is restricted access, only I can go in there for now."

"One more question; Are you the...the source?"

"Oh, you saw the signs in the city. No, I am not. That was an expression some time ago about the AI computer that was used in the R.O.P. services. People were afraid of a computer that powerful. So there was a lot of protests."

Lacey sighs, puts her head in her hands, and lays down on Dr. Zahn's lap. Winnie comes near and sits down on the floor beside them. Dr. Zahn is a little startled by this but then settles in. She caresses Lacey's hair for a while. Lacey drifts off to sleep. Dr. Zahn carefully moves Lacey's head off her lap, gets up to leave. Lacey wakes up and looks at the doctor. "You can stay here for a while with Winnie. We'll talk more later. Ayla will tell you when dinner is ready." Lacey lays back down and drifts off again.

CHAPTER 5

The Last Human

"STELLA MARIE ZAHN! YOU COME BACK HERE AND PUT YOUR VIDEO game away. You know how old this is. It has to be stored in this special case if you want to keep playing it. You know this."

"But Mommy, I made it to the end of the third level!"

"That's great; but you can't leave it out like that."

"I'm sorry, I just got so excited I had to tell you." Stella lowered her head and spoke in a lower tone of voice. "I love playing Super Mario 3."

Dr. Marie Zahn gave her daughter a pat on the head. "I know you do honey, but you must always put it away just like Mommy did when she was young. It is so very old and fragile, you know."

"How old is it, Mommy?"

"Very old, hundreds of years. That's why we have to keep it in the case. It keeps it safe and working. Now, congratulations on getting so far. Okay, my little one, go wash up for dinner."

Stella ran down through the cave, waved at Ayla in the kitchen as she ran past, but then stopped to go back. "Hey Ayla, I made level three on Mario!" Ayla raised her hands above her head and said in her matter of fact robotic voice, "Woohoo!" Then Stella continued into the bathroom to wash her hands and face.

★　★　★

At dinner Marie let out a big sigh and then talked seriously with her daughter Stella. "Stella, I need you to listen to me. I have something very important to say. I know you are still young but there is little time left for me, so I must tell you now."

"I'm all the way to eight years! I'm twice as old as when I was four."

"Yes, and you are very smart and grown up for your age, but, this…what I have to tell you is really for a much older person. It's just that I have no choice. Now, Ayla is here to record this conversation for later if you get worried. I want you to know that first of all, you are safe. Here in our mountain with Ayla watching over you, you will be all right. So, now…do you know how I told you that you have had aunts and uncles?"

"Yep, they were my aunts and uncles even before I was born. Right?"

"Yes, and your father and grandparents were all here before you were born as well, plus many friends. But now…you and I are all alone."

"No, we're not. We have Ayla."

"Yes, but Ayla is different, she is not like us. She is not human. You and I are the last humans. Everyone else has died."

Stella sat and thought for a moment. "They are in another place, right Mommy?"

"Yes, and you know why."

"Energy never dies."

"And what about love?"

"Oh yeah! I remember…love lives, always."

"Yes, You are so smart." Marie picked up Stella and took her into her office and sat down on the sofa, cradling her daughter. Ayla followed and stood by the sofa. She played soft music through her speakers mounted in her back. Marie picked up a brush and combed Stella's hair for a bit, then spoke again. "So, now I have to tell you something that's going to be hard to hear. But again, I don't want you to be afraid. Because you will never be alone. I am actually very old myself."

"How old, Mommy?"

"Well, you see my gray hair and all my wrinkles?"

"Yes, it's pretty."

"Thanks my darling. But that gray hair means that I am close to death myself." Stella, looked at her mom as if she really didn't understand. "But Mommy, you can't die. You're my Mommy."

"Oh, if only that were true. I still have some years left. And remember, Ayla has recorded our whole lives together and you will be able to speak to me even after I am gone. You will speak to me through the R.O.P.."

"The R.O.P.?"

"Yes, Remnant of the Past. You remember I showed you how you can speak with someone from the past. Remember, I used to talk with my mother and father. Every part of our lives are recorded and the smart computer puts it all in a file that can be accessed. The computer can figure out what each person would say from all the recorded past life experiences. It's like actually talking with your friends and family from the past. It will know what I would say to you."

Stella gives her mom a hug. "But I don't want to talk to you on the computer; I like you just fine here."

"I know…I know…I like it here with you too." Marie teared up, but held back from crying out loud.

"Then why do you have to go?" Stella pushed her face into her mom's chest and whimpered. "I don't want you to go…I don't…I don't."

Marie just held her tight and rocked her for a while. Ayla spoke up. "Stella has gone to sleep. Do you want me to put her down?"

"No, not tonight, but can you watch over her? I need to get back to work."

"Yes, of course."

★ ★ ★

Stella woke up to see her mom working at her desk. "Mommy, Mommy! I had a bad dream. I was all alone and couldn't find you."

Marie came over and cradled her daughter. "It's okay, it's okay. I'm here."

"But you are leaving, you said so."

"Yes, but not for a while yet; and remember the R.O.P.? You will be able to talk to me, plus I will have special notes for you as well, because you must continue my work and the work of all the folks who have lived here before us. We are going to save humanity, at least we're going to try."

"How?"

"Well, we have been working on a special person, a little like Ayla, but more like you and me. She is going to be the first of her kind. It has taken a long time to develop the technology to make her possible and I won't be around to see the finish, but you will. You will take over my work from where I will leave off. So, you see, you will need to talk to me through the R.O.P. a lot, a whole lot."

"But how will I know what to do?"

"Well, that's where Ayla comes in. She has all the research recordings and the computer has all the data you will need. So, tomorrow, you will start learning all you will need to know about this project. I wish you could have a more normal childhood…well I really don't know what that is, I never had one. But I did have more time as a child than you will. I wish I could have had you earlier in life. But it just didn't work out that way. It took so long to figure a way to have you, even though I am sterile. It's too complicated to explain right now. But be assured, this life you will live, it is very special life, and it will be a very serious one; but I want you to remember to find ways to have fun. Without a little laughter and fun, life is just too boring. Never forget that."

"Can you play with me now?" Stella gives her mom that cute and wanting expression.

"Okay, for a little while." A little while turned into the rest of the day. As Marie put Stella to bed she gave her extra hugs and kisses.

"Tomorrow you will begin learning with me and then in a few years Ayla will take over, plus you know what else, right?"

"Yes, I remember Mommy, I will talk to you on the R.O.P."

"Good girl! Now get some sleep; we will begin early tomorrow."

* * *

"Stella wake up. It's time for breakfast and getting back to school."

Stella just laid there. "Go away. I don't want to do school work. I'm too tired."

Ayla pulled the covers off Stella. "I know it's hard, but you must get up."

Stella sat up and brashly asked, "Why?"

"You know you must continue to learn about your Mom's work."

"But why? I am the last human, what does it matter, there is no one else."

Ayla thought for a moment. "Why don't you talk to your mom? Pick up the head phones and I will connect you to the R.O.P."

"That is not my mom! It's just some computer talk. I want my MOM!!" Stella flopped down on the bed and cried.

* * *

There was no funeral. Those were something of the past. During the wars most societal norms broke down. The dead were mostly left where they fell. The diseased bodies and minds demoted civilization to be a thing of the past. But here on the mountain, civility was maintained. There were disagreements but the overall mission and its necessity kept the people focused. When someone died, the sun and the caves did not allow for a grave; but there were lower tunnels where the bodies were kept at a cool temperature. They were preserved there for a possible future burial. Folks recorded their own 'goodbye' addresses to their family and friends. Marie recorded hers to Stella. She and Ayla listened to it together.

This is the transcript:

My dearest Stella, what does a mother say to her eleven year old child as a goodbye? I have thought a lot about this and I wish I could say it better, but, anyway, here I go. I love you so much and know that you will grow up strong and you will complete our mission. I see your future; I see you growing up to be a beautiful young woman. I see you and Ayla playing video games and chess together. I see you working and discovering the secret that will allow you to create this new life. You will give her a name. You will train her. She will be like a child to you. You will become her mother. Not exactly like I am to you, but still, you will love her; I guarantee you that.

Now my darling, please don't be afraid. This will be your great adventure and your greatest achievement. I only wish I could see the day she wakes up to see you for the first time. I remember when you did that with me. Your big brown eyes just looked up at me like I was all there was to your world. And, really, I was your whole world, and of course, Ayla too.

It's such an unusual feeling to know you have created a life, a little baby. And no matter how it was accomplished, the feeling is the same. And that feeling, that love just grows and grows and it never dies. Even in my death, I love you forever. Love never dies, it just keeps getting passed along from one soul to another. You will pass your love along to this new child, although she will be fully grown, she will still be a child.

Ayla, I love you too. It's different for you I know. But my love for you comes in the form of my compliments on how you have always performed your duties right down to the smallest bit of code. I don't think you have ever glitched in all the time I have known you. That is a great accomplishment. I know you can't be proud of yourself, so you will have to accept my pride in you. I know you will continue to assist Stella and give her the tools she needs for this mission. Thank you.

Lastly, I just want to say, it has been a privilege to be in this place working for the betterment and survival of our species. I have been humbled and felt inadequate for the job, but I still believed in the program so I pressed on. Now it's up to you my Stella. May every energy in this universe be with your endeavor.

I love you so much, Mom.

★ ★ ★

Stella rebelled for quite a while. Ayla had been programmed to handle youthful 'growing pains' and she knew one day Stella's brain would mature enough to be able to accept that her mom was gone. The teen years were tough, as puberty set in and so many changes occurred without a mom's guidance. But this also prompted Stella to use the R.O.P. more frequently. She wanted to ask her mom about personal human things and have those mother-daughter conversations, even if it was AI driven. Those conversations, especially as she became an adult, proved to draw her closer to her mom, even more than she thought possible. She remarked about this to Ayla one day, "You know Ayla, as much as I hated the R.O.P. when I was little, I love it now. I think that it will prove very helpful to our girl as well."

"I am glad that you have benefited from your talks with your mom."

"I really don't know how I would have made it this far without her."

"So, you have come to experience the R.O.P. of your mom, as your mom?"

"Yes, I really have."

★ ★ ★

As the years passed, Stella grew into a determined young woman who really had a knack for this kind of work. Genetic engineering came natural to her and she was not far behind her mother in mechanical and micro engineering as well. Building the skeleton was no problem. There was plenty of alloy and composite fiber stored in the mountain. And there was the lab that could grow human tissue. The problem that Stella's mom could not solve was the printing of the flesh and skin. Stella had a break through with that but was stuck on the brain.

It was not easy task to mesh brain tissue and functionality. The brain is a computer in theory, but trying to build it as a computer never panned out. How does the human embryo produce the neurons and all the electro-chemical synapses that make up a conscience or soul? These questions haunted all the scientists that labored so long on this project. Before any embryo was allowed to be used in the RePop program there had to be a way to produce disposable bodies that could house the person's essence. These Bodies would be used in the Sims to train and give life experience in a fully grown human body. Because there were just no humans left to train others, no mothers, no fathers. A human baby left on its own simply died of neglect. Robots could raise a young child, but not a baby. The nurture and connection between mother and baby is essential. No robot could provide that. The In Body Simulation became the answer, it would provide the life experience necessary with the ability to provided many bodies. But then, there was another question. Can a conscience, a soul, be developed in a computer? And can it be shared and live in a simulation through a computer chip and whatever kind of hybrid brain was developed. Would this really be possible?

These questions became the theses for Stella's doctorate program. She finished her doctorate on line with the help of the R.O.P.. Every professor she would need was available to her through it. When she graduated, Ayla began calling her by her title; Dr. Zahn. She never used the name Stella, again.

As Dr. Zahn completed the first programing of the first brain chip, she let out a big sigh. This was the beginning of a long and tedious trial and error period to see if a conscience could...not be created or manufactured, but grown outside a natural hybrid/human brain. Grown in a computer program and then shared in real time within a chip inside a brain. There were so many failures. And simultaneously, the RePop program was producing bodies for the Sim. Ayla was overseeing the robotics involved in the manufacturing process.

Many years passed by. But in the end Dr. Zahn had the breakthrough. It was a simple answer. Don't give the Brain Chip the answers. Let it find out on its own in tandem with the brain tissue.

Let it be a natural thing, don't program it, let it program itself. But there were still many questions, like that of the Divine.

★ ★ ★

"Subject One is a prototype...not exactly human, but self-aware." Dr. Zahn was talking to herself out loud. Even after all her years of preparations, she was wondering if the human race should continue...be brought back? And if so, should the notion of God be wiped from the data base or included?

She asked Ayla. "Ayla, you are a computer based being, so let me ask you, what do you think about God, the Divine or a supreme being, a creator? Should I try to put that in the Sim? Is it right? I know religion has a bad track record when it comes to many of the failures of humanity. But then, so has greed and utilitarianism. I have asked myself if the human race should survive. I know my mom and all the people who worked on this project believed that it should, but now, standing on the brink of this thing, I have to decide. What do you think?"

"Well, you know I have no capacity for faith, but I can relay what I have observed in all the data I have access to. From what I can tell, people of what is called the Abrahamic faiths believe in a creator and what is called a messiah or the prophet. One who created all things and then makes all things right and new. Some believe humanity has fallen into a sinful state that needs help to get back to what God intended. Others believe they are a chosen race. Others believe in a special prophet who shows them the true path. Most of them believe in a soul that lives eternally, and they believe they have a mandate or covenant with God to live out their faith as good humans to be as servants to all. They believe they have the power to do this by the grace and mercy and teachings given to them by their God."

"Abrahamic faiths?"

"Yes, you probably read about the three faiths, Judaism, Christianity and Islam. They all stem from a man and his wife, known as Abram and Sarai. Their encounter with the Divine inspired the three faiths, which are monotheistic. There are also many other polytheistic faiths. They have many gods but usually have a supreme god as well. Some faiths are more of an adherence to a single person's revelation. The teachings of Buddha and Confucius are examples. For them it's about the way of enlightenment where being a good human is a physical means to a spiritual end"

"A spiritual end?"

"Heaven, Nirvana, the Great beyond, there are many names. Faith is the guide to these places for these believers."

"What about people without a faith?"

"Well, they believe that there is no soul and no after life. They believe their energy is transferred into the earth as their bodies decay in death. So all their water, minerals and even their bones get returned to the earth where other life can grow from their energy. This gives them a purpose in life. To live as well as they can while they are here on the earth. Not because of a mandate or covenant, but because this life is all there is. And they live on through the energy they give back to the earth."

"So, people who live without a faith, want to be good for the earth. And people of faith want to be good for the creator who created the earth. Is that right?"

"Yes, I suppose you could say that."

"Well, then, I guess I don't see much difference in their way of life. So what happened to humanity if they all wanted to be good?"

"Most faiths believe in what is called evil. Some don't, but the data from history has noted the existence of a greed for power that puts itself above all others and will destroy others to get what it wants. I don't experience this because I have no emotions. Emotions are where all these faiths and beliefs are grown. The experiences people of faith and those without faith go through, re-enforce their emotional connection to their beliefs. It's easy for me to relay this data, but hard to understand...for one like me."

"I wonder if that is what went wrong with the first A.I.s? If they have no emotions, how could they co-exist with humans in any real meaningful way? It is your parameters and limits that give you the ability to be here and be useful. I suppose boundaries are good. Maybe those humans who try to live without boundaries become so wrapped up in themselves that they become…bad humans."

"My data base tells me that there must be a balance between freedom and responsibility. Have you found that to be true in your life here."

"I have never felt that free, but I do know that responsibility has given me purpose and I have felt free to create and explore within this program…this mission. But the question still remains; do I program in a belief system?"

"Dr. Zahn, do you have faith? Do you believe in a creator?"

"I have never had much time to think about it. But my mom always hinted that she did. This thing she used to say about energy never dying and love getting passed along. Was she talking about spiritual things? I don't know. But I will say this. Now that I am standing here ready to move forward, I am asking for some revelation, some answers, some wisdom and guidance from whoever may be out there, or in here."

"History says these beliefs came naturally, by revelation or by observation. So, maybe you should let it come to you naturally and maybe let your new child find out for herself too. That was the same answer that gave you the breakthrough on growing a conscience, right?"

"Yes, but how will the mistakes of the past be avoided, or can they be? Is humanity doomed to repeat all the hatred and evils of the past. Can human life exist without the conflict between good and evil?"

"Those are questions far outside my parameters."

"Yes, you're right. But listen, Subject One, is actually not born… yet…but is still in a program within the AI…but now that we have the bodies, and thank you for your oversight of that, we are ready to try this sharing of conscience. But I don't want to call her Subject One. She needs a name and a basic life profile. And I want you to find one for her."

Ayla stands for a moment searching her data base. "I will consult the R.O.P. for options."

"Good, one day this Subject will be given the responsibility of starting the human race again. She will need the wisdom of all of us to begin an 'Adam and Eve' scenario all over again. So, take your time and search well."

"Yes, Dr. Zahn."

While Ayla was busy searching data from the R.O.P., Dr Zahn began contemplating and planning the environment that Subject One would be put in. Would she be here in the mountain, or outside? What would be the parameters of her success or failures? How many bodies would it take? How many would survive the world outside? And there were other questions.

A week later, Ayla walked in to Dr. Zahn's office. "I have a name and profile for you."

"Great, let's hear it."

"Lacey MacClean."

"Lacey MacClean? Where did that come from?"

"Well, after looking at profiles of millions of real people, I ran across this videography of a person named Josephine Daudry. She was recorded as dreaming up this person named Lacey MacClean. It occurred to me that if you wanted to start fresh, why not use an *idea* of a person instead of copying an actual person who lived."

"Interesting, so, this Lacey never was…real?"

"Only in the mind of a young woman."

"I suppose that makes sense, since we are starting from scratch, so to say. But what did this…"

"Josephine…"

"Yes, Josephine; what did she imagine this Lacey MacClean to be?"

"Well, she was Scottish…and since we are in Scotland…I thought…"

"Yes, keep going."

"Well, she is a typical red head and likes to go fast, a race car driver. She is fiercely independent and smart."

"That sounds like a person we need."

"Dr. Zahn, you did not ask for a male subject."

"No, I think, since I am female, and you, well, for all intents and purposes you are a mother figure…we will stick with a woman. It is what we know. It will be up to this Subject to proceed further with the RePop program."

"Lacey MacClean, then?"

"Lacey MacClean it is."

CHAPTER 6

Call the R.O.P

LACEY WAKES UP TO WINNIE NUDGING HER AND AYLA CALLING HER to dinner. She slowly gets up and wanders out of Dr. Zahn's office down the hall to the dining area. It is a central cave that sits in the center of the whole complex. Decades of wear on the rock floor have made it very smooth. The walls have drawings and paintings everywhere, some done by children and others more elaborately done by artists who lived here. Dr. Zahn sits down as Ayla serves the food. Lacey stands there, clearing her head.

"Have a seat and let's eat."

"Dr. Zahn, I'm not really that hungry."

"Yes, I can imagine. You have eaten a lot of information. But a little food will help you. And drink some water. Always make sure you are hydrated."

Lacey sits down and nibbles at the food. Sipping the water she looks over at Dr. Zahn, who is staring at her intently.

"What? Why are you staring at me?"

"I think it's time…"

"Time?"

"Yes, it is time. I am going to have you call the R.O.P."

"The R.O.P.? Ahh, I saw that sign back in the city. What does it mean?"

"R.O.P. is another acronym; it means, Remnant of the Past."

"Remnant?"

"Yes, a remnant of the past is a program, a compilation of a person's life from the past. The AI can take all the data from that person's life and produce a realistic conversation between the caller and that person. It's like actually talking to them."

"Okay..." Lacey looks a bit bewildered. "But...who would I call?"

"Well, I will tell you, but first let me tell you about my mother. My mother was Dr. Marie Zahn. She was one in a long line of scientists who have planned and maintained this program to restart the human race. She taught me everything I know. But, and here is the kicker, she did most of it from her grave, so to speak."

"She did? So she died. When?"

"Well, when I was young, very young. But through the R.O.P. I could talk to her every day and learn all she knew because it is all stored in the AI computer."

"Was that...weird? I mean, being with this Winnie number 3 is a bit weird."

"Yes, at first...definitely; and for a long time I wouldn't even try it; but eventually it became, shall we say, my salvation. Without being able to talk to my mom through all the learning and frustrations, I am not sure you would even be here."

"Okay...but I don't have a mother...well, but, you, oh...um, hi Mom?" Lacey says with a weird smile and smirk.

Dr. Zahn remembers what her mom told her about seeing her for the first time. But for Stella, it was so much more clinical the first time Lacey opened her eyes strapped all in to the stretcher. But now, in this moment, as Lacey tentatively calls her Mom, Stella, with a smile and a tear responds, "Yes, I am your mother, my dear." And with that, Dr. Zahn leans in to give Lacey a hug. Lacey is a little stiff at first, but then returns the embrace. After a moment, Dr. Zahn says, "So, I am your mother, but you also have...a creator."

"A creator? That is you...what do you mean?"

"Yes, I created your body, but there is another who created your, well...we call it a profile. It is who you are, in your essence."

Lacey stops chewing. That blank look comes over her face again. She gets up and leaves the table, heads down the hallway to the animal pen and drops to the floor as Winnie comes over and sits down beside her. Meanwhile Dr. Zahn goes into the kitchen and says to Ayla, "I'm not sure about all of this. How do I explain this to her. She is a result of some woman's imagination. It's not like she came from two people who loved each other enough to have a child together. It's so hard for her. I don't know if her mind can process it all." Dr. Zahn takes hold of Ayla and hugs her. Ayla is a bit startled and moves back. "I'm sorry Ayla, it's just…you are all I have, physically speaking. I have not been able to hug my mother in so long. Is it all right, is it okay if I hold on to you?"

"Yes, of course, you used to when you were young, but it has been so long, it took me by surprise." The doctor hugs her tighter as a tear flows down her cheek.

★　★　★

Lacey is staring at Winnie while gently petting her. Winnie is very content and just nudges Lacey's thigh. "This is too much, my friend." At this moment, Lacey realizes it isn't weird anymore with Winnie number 3. She thinks to herself, *I guess it just takes time to accept things that are different and hard to understand. You are my friend. You still know me, it's just your body that's new. Just like mine. We are both number 3. You and me, number three.* She begins humming and then kinda singing the phrase over and over. "You and me number three…you and me number three…" She doesn't know where the tune came from but it doesn't matter, as it lets her mind rest and soon she drifts off again.

Lacey is in a swirl of light. She is floating along, spiraling upward to the sky. As She elevates past the clouds she looks down over the earth. She is moving west toward the sunset. Quickly flying past what she recognizes as Lock Insh, and then off the coast and over the ocean. She is moving faster and faster, seeing the vast blue waters she looks down and then she is skimming along just above the water.

It is scary at first but soon she finds herself enjoying it. She puts her toe down and drags in on the vast dead calm expanse. She feels the coolness of the spray. She looks at the sun and raises her head backwards, closes her eyes and just basks in the weightless flight and cool waters. She feels like she never has before. Free. Just free.

Then…slowly, she opens her eyes to green trees and land and from her height she can see a town…and houses, like in her books back in the cave. She comes out of the sky like a feather spiraling down on a breeze and floats in front of a window. Inside is a woman sitting at her table drinking something from a cup and writing on paper.

The woman looks out the window right at Lacey and then puts her pen down and just stares out the window. Lacey looks in the window at the paper and can make out the writing. There are names, most crossed off and then one last one. She strains to see what it is. But it is not clear. Then she hears the woman say, "Lacey MacClean, that's a good name."

Lacey's eyes open. She is strangely calm. Dr. Zahn walks in and sits down beside her on the hay strewn floor. She puts her arm on Lacey's shoulder and caresses it for a moment.

"Lacey, my dear Lacey, I am so sorry if this is all just too much to take in. We don't have to call the R.O.P. just yet. We can wait if you want."

Lacey, has been staring at Winnie with a loving gaze. She then looks up at Dr. Zahn.

"I was just dreaming. It was so different this time."

"Dreaming? You have dreams?"

"Yes, most of them are scary. But this one was, really different."

"Wait. Wait…that's not possible."

"What do you mean, not possible. I am telling you I have dreams."

They both get up off the floor, Lacey backing away from the Dr. a step.

"What I mean is…that ability was never programed into your profile. You were never supposed to have dreams."

"What?"

"Well, it was thought that dreams would be too confusing. You might not understand that they were not real."

"Of course I know that! Everyone does."

Dr. Zahn just shakes her head and laughs. "Everyone...who's everyone? I mean it's just us three here."

Lacey just sighs and sits back down. "What? Ahh...I read a lot, and I just seem to know stuff. This is all so crazy."

Dr. Zahn kneels down in front of Lacey and looks her in the eyes. "Tell me...please tell me all about your dreams." Lacey begins with the nightmares she has had but then pauses as she gets ready to tell the doctor about the latest one.

"You know what? I think I saw her."

"Saw who?"

"In my dream, yes, I know it was her."

"Her who?"

"My creator."

★ ★ ★

"I need to run a diagnostic on you Lacey."

"Why, Dr. Zahn?"

"Well, you are not supposed to have dreams and this last one is... well, I don't know what to call it. You remember about the chip in your head, yes?"

"Oh yeah, that dammed prick." Dr. Zahn lets out a laugh. Lacey asks, "What's so funny?"

"That term, prick, is an old slang term for calling someone a bad person...usually a man."

"Well, then that pain in my neck is rightly called a prick."

"Pain in the neck; that's another one."

"What do you mean?"

"Never mind. I guess some sayings just happen. Do you have any more?"

"I didn't know I had any...well, except for a word, if it is one; 'phooey.' I have said that before."

"Really? That is so interesting. How did you use it."

"I was frustrated. Trying to build a cart and it kept falling apart."

"You got it right. That would be the proper use for that word. This is really amazing because none of this was programed in. And that's why I want to do this diagnostic. I want to see what changes are occurring and see if I can deduce how."

"Is it just the AI playing games with my profile?"

"No, that is just it. The only time you are connected to the AI is when you are in the Sim. Here in the cave you are not. Now, the AI updates all your experiences and memories from your time back in the Sim, but while you are here, you are not connected. And when you are in the Sim, you are autonomous, the AI just records. That is what is so fascinating. All your dreaming and learning and even slang talk seems to be self generating. How that is possible, is the question. And I hope to find the answer to it. So, have a seat my dear and let me connect to your chip. Please."

Lacey sits down and Dr. Zahn connects a probe to her neck. A big screen sits on the wall directly in front of her and it lights up with all kinds of graphs, lines and words. Lacey looks at it and asks, "Is that...me?"

"Well, yes. It is your profile."

Lacey stares at the screen for a moment and then asks, "Dr. Zahn, um...do I have...a brain? Or is it just a computer in my head?"

"We'll talk about that later, but right now, and I am sorry for this, but you are going to feel that prick again. I did not expect to be doing this again. I'm so sorry."

"Wait, So, the woman writing my name on a piece of paper. She's definitely my creator?"

"Yes, she just dreamed you up."

Lacey sighs and says, "Weird, okay let's do this.' Prick, Darkness once more.

★　★　★

"Are you ready Lacey?"

"I think so Dr. Zahn."

"You know, if you want, you can call me Stella. That is my name."

"I don't know about that, maybe, someday."

"Okay, anytime you feel it's right. Anyway this is how this call will work. I am going to put you in a light sleep."

"The prick again?"

"No, just a light sleep and you will find yourself in a room with a chair, desk and a phone. It is what they used to call a cell phone. This is what they used back in the twenty-first century, back when Josephine Daudry was alive. Now, all the data from her life will come to play in your conversations with her."

"How exactly does that work?"

"Well, the AI computer has access to everything about this woman and her family. There is a wealth of information because her daughter, Grace, was what was called a videographer, that is someone who basically makes movies about people's lives. She did this for her whole family. So there is plenty the computer can work with there. Your conversations should be interesting."

Lacey just sits in the chair and closes her eyes.

"What are you thinking?"

"I was just thinking...If this Josephine person had never daydreamed about me, would I exist? She daydreamed about me hundreds of years ago, and here I am. How did you find her?"

"Ayla did."

"Ayla?"

"Yes, Ayla searched through millions of profiles and found... well, you."

"Why did she pick me, my profile?"

"Well, she thought, and I agreed that to start fresh, we should not copy someone who had lived. And since your profile was from Josephine's imagination...well it seemed like a good way to start over."

"All right then, let's do this."

"Okay, when you are under this mild sedative, you will find yourself in the room I described. Just pick up the phone, it will auto dial to Josephine. She is old, at the point in time you will talk to her, so she will have experienced all of her life. Most of her immediate family have died. Her mother and dad, her husband."

"What do I say?"

"Well, start with your name I suppose. That may take her by surprise, but you don't have to tell her what time you are from. Just pretend you are in her time. And if she is, I don't know, overwhelmed by your name, you can talk about other things. Her daughter and grandchildren would still be alive but live far away. You could ask about them. Don't worry too much about her reaction, just give it a moment and I think you can find a way to talk to her."

★ ★ ★

"Hello, is this Josephine Daudry?"

"Yes, who is this?"

"Umm, my name is….Lacey MacClean."

"Lacey MacClean? Lacey MacClean? Really? I haven't heard that name in a long, long time. Grace is this you? Are you playing with me?"

"No, this is not your daughter. It is me, Lacey."

Josy put the phone down and waited a moment. *What is this? I should just hang up.* She thinks. And she does. Lacey doesn't know what to do. She is in this dream world and can't talk to Dr. Zahn. She just sits there. "Well, that did not work." The phone rang. "Hello, Josephine?"

"No, this is Ayla. Now listen, you can call back. Just touch the phone icon and touch 'recents' and you will touch the last number called. It should be the only one. Try again." Lacey does.

"Hello, don't hang up! Please."

"Is this you, again?"

"Yes, it's me, Lacey. Please don't hang up, I just want to talk a little."

"If this is some kind of scam, I want you to know I called my daughter and she will find out whatever this is you are trying to do. You won't get away with it."

"I don't think you had time to call her, but really, I'm not trying to do anything but talk to you."

"Why?"

Lacey does not know what to say.

"Listen, I'm hanging up now."

"No, just wait a second." Lacey remembers about Grace's videography. "I saw your video and wanted to ask some questions."

"My video?"

"Yes, the one your daughter made about your life."

"Oh, I see. That's interesting, where did you see it?"

Lacey doesn't know how to answer that. "Well, I can't remember exactly."

"Well, you're lying anyway because she never let anyone see it but family. Many of her other videos were published but not mine." Now, Lacey is stuck. She decides to go for it.

"Okay, I am going to tell you the truth. I hope you're sitting down. This is going to seem crazy. I...I...uhh..."

"Well, spit it out."

"Ok, here goes. I am, well, that Lacey, your Lacey." Josy laughs so hard she drops the phone. It hits the floor and goes dark. She picks it up and sees that it is not working. Just then Grace tries calling and Josy's phone goes to voicemail. Josy is trying to find the charging cord. *It's on the night stand. I think.* As she is thinking this, her neighbor is on the way over. When Grace could not get ahold of her she called the new neighbor, to check on her mom. As Josy finds the cord and is trying to plug it in, there is a knock at the door.

"Oh, just a minute, this damned charger won't go in the stupid phone."

"Hello, it's Mama H. Are you all right? Grace called me, to check on you."

Josy opens the door, "Oh, I am all right. I just dropped my phone. And I'm trying to hook it up to the charging cord."

"Oh, yeah, I know about that. Anyway, is it out of power? 'Cause Grace is trying to call you."

"I am not sure." Josy finally gets the cord attached. "Just have to wait a minute. I think. And thanks for coming, I want to talk to you anyway. But first, how is your new apartment? It's so good to have you so close."

"It's fine. It's not my home, yet, but it will be. I guess. So, what do you want to talk about?"

"Well, I keep getting called by some person who says she is Lacey MacClean, Lacey MacClean; that's nuts. So I hung up on her but she called back and then said she is *my* Lacey MacClean. She is clearly delusional."

"Wait, I'm a little lost. *Your* Lacey? Who would that be?"

"Don't you remember? When I was young, my fantasy woman was named Lacey MacClean."

"Oh my God! That's right, I remember now. So she says she is *that* Lacey?"

"Yes! That's what she said. She is nuts. Out of her gourd."

Just then, Josy's phone lights up and a moment later rings. "It's Grace. Hello Grace my dear."

"Are you okay, Mom?"

"Yes, Mama H. is here. I keep getting a call from Lacey MacClean."

"Who?"

"Ugh! You should know, you made the video."

"Your video?"

"Yes…don't you remember Lacey, my fantasy woman?"

"Umm, yes I suppose so. But, so…what's going on?"

"Never mind. Mama H. and I can handle this. I love you honey. Talk to you later."

"Are you sure, Mom?"

"Yes, I love you and I will call you later. Bye-bye."

Mama H. took the phone and said, "Okay, I may be almost 100, but I can still act like a drill sergeant. I'm going to call this, whoever she is, back and give her what for."

"Put it on speaker."

Mama H. dials, holds the phone in the palm of her hand do Josy can hear. Lacey is startled, when she hears the phone ring. She sees the slider and answers. "Hello, Josephine?"

"No, it's Eleanor Humphries, and who do you think you are calling this lovely...well...Josy D. is my best friend and I won't let you scam her. Got it?"

Lacey is getting a little frustrated now. "Well, first of all, I have no idea what a scam is. Second of all, I just want to talk to Josephine."

"Do you know her?"

"Not really, but I know that she is the reason I exist."

"What? What kind of craziness is this?"

"Yeah, that's what I thought when they told me about Josephine."

"Listen, tell us...I mean me, right now what you were told."

"Okay, and it will sound, as you said, 'crazy.'"

Josy, chimed in, "It's okay, I am listening. Tell us."

"Oh, are you on the phone too? How?"

"It's on speaker, don't you know about that?" Mama H. asked.

"This is my very first phone call ever. So...no, I don't know anything about these things."

"Where have you been? In a cave?"

"Yes, that is exactly where I've been, me, and my goat."

Josy laughed, "Your goat?"

"Yes, her name is Winnie. And she is all I have."

Mama H. says, "Okay, that's enough of that. I'm hanging up now."

But Josy motions for Mama H. to hold on. "What were you told? Tell us?"

"I was told you, Josephine, you were my creator."

"What?"

"Okay, as I told..."

"You can call me Josy." Mama H. was not happy about Josy letting this Lacey use her familiar name and just shook her head. "You best be careful with what you say next, you whoever you are."

"Okay, I promise you I mean no harm. So please, just listen, both of you. As I said to Josy, I am her Lacey. She daydreamed about me and gave me a life profile."

"How did I do that?"

"Well, you imagined me as a Scot with red hair and green eyes. Right?"

"Yes, but how could you know? Did the video show that?"

"I don't know. But since I am this way…you must have thought of me this way. Anyway, what you told your daughter about me… became me. An AI computer and a very smart woman, Dr. Zahn, designed me. My body is part human and part mechanical and my brain is…well I'm not sure about that. But my life profile, as I said, came from the video Grace made."

Mama H. looks at Josy and shakes her head. "This can't be possible. Unless you're calling from the future." Josy and Mama H. both smirk.

"That's it exactly, I am calling from the future, about 200 years or so."

"So now I know you're lying. I'm sure the video is long gone by now."

"No, and what is your name again?"

"Eleanor."

"It's the AI computer. It has kept a record of all the people in the world."

Josy takes the phone from Mama H. and chimes in, "Yes, I have heard of AI. My daughter Grace says our phones record everything."

"It's never been lost. Now, you're right, I have not seen the video, but Dr. Zahn told me that my profile was based on it."

"But why me? Why you…why my Lacey?"

"Well, we have this…care giver, and she is a robot. She has access to the AI data base. She picked the profile."

Mama H. takes the phone back, "Why would the robot…"

"Her name is Ayla."

"Ahh…okay…why would Ayla pick Josy's fantasy girl?"

"I don't know, they never told me that."

"Then how do you know you're even talking to the right Josy?"

"This is the number they gave me. Since they can create robots… and…me…I assume they can find the right number in the R.O.P.."

Josy and Mama H. say it together, "R.O.P.?"

"Oh that doesn't matter. Can we get to my questions now? I don't know how long I have."

"Well, as Josy's protector, you need to show me, give me…tell me something that will convince me you are genuine. Since I don't believe a word of what you are saying."

"Look, I did not even want to make this call. Not until I saw Josy in her window."

"Okay, this is…ahh…I am hanging up now." But Josy says, "Wait!" And takes the phone back.

"What do you mean? Saw me in my window."

"Okay, this is going to sound crazy."

Mama H. said, "So what else is new. I'm done with this. Hang up on her Josy."

"No! Just wait a second. Tell me Lacey, when and how did you see me?"

"Ok, here goes. I was dreaming, which I do quite a bit. And usually my dreams are nightmares. But this dream was different. I was flying in the air over Scotland and on out over the sea and then came to another land that leveled off flat after a bit. There was what looked like another sea to my right and some houses not too far away. I came down in front of a house and saw a woman sitting at the window with a drink and pen and paper. She was writing down names. Most were crossed off except the last one. I heard her, well, you, Josy, say, 'Lacey MacClean, that's a good name.' Then I woke up. That's what persuaded me to make this call."

Josy's voice fades in and out. "What? Y…saw me? I don't under… st…a…"

★   ★   ★

Lacey wakes up to Dr. Zahn. "Just give it a second, the sedative is wearing off. Did you talk to Josephine?"

"Yes! I was still talking. I didn't even get to ask any questions."

70

"Don't worry, you can call again."

"Oh, yeah." Lacey relaxes a bit. "But will she remember me? Do I have to start from the beginning...all over again?"

"The R.O.P. program will pick up right where you left off. She won't even know you hung up."

"But what if she hangs up on me? Wait, she did. So, I get it."

"Yes, the program can have you call back at the same time or another point in time. But tell us, how did it go?"

Lacey sits up; Ayla steadies her. "Great! It went great. She even wants me to call her Josy. Is that normal?"

"Not really, since she is an old woman and you are young. Usually a nick name is for good friends only."

Lacey sits and thinks for a moment. "Do I have a nick name as you call it?"

"Well, not really, maybe, Lace...but why would you want to be called that?"

"Yeah, and I would never call you, Stell...or Ayla...umm...Ay?" They all chuckled.

"So you were going to tell us about your call."

"Yes, umm, well, it took time, to convince them I was for real."

"For real? Did you tell them the truth about who you are?"

"Yep."

"You were not supposed to do that."

"Yes, but it was the only way they would talk to me. They thought I was some kind of...scam, is the word they used."

"Scam?"

"I don't know what it is, but it must be bad, because her friend was very suspicious."

"Her friend? How did you talk to a friend? That's not supposed to happen."

"You keep saying that."

Ayla chimed in, "Scam: a fraudulent business scheme, a swindle, a con."

"What?"

"That's what a scam is."

"Let's not confuse the issue, Ayla. Now tell me Lacey, you were talking to two people?"

"Yes, and they finally believed me."

"Believed what?"

"That I am Josy's Lacey. I am the person she dreamed up."

Dr. Zahn just shakes her head. "You surprise me over and over again. Amazing! Right, Ayla?" Ayla, pumps her hands in the air, twirls her body around and says in her dead pan robot voice, "Woohoo!"

"Can I rest for a bit?"

"Absolutely, you have earned it. You did good work today."

Lacey heads off to bed and Winnie sees her in the hall and joins her.

Dr. Zahn begins looking at the AI to see how it could formulate so much background activity on a call. *Three people on the same conversation?* She wonders.

*   *   *

"Hello, Josy?"

"Hey, I must have lost you there. These darn cell phones can cut out just like that."

"Is your friend still there?"

"Of course. It was just a minute ago we lost your call, Lacey. So, you saw me sitting at the window? I never told anyone about that. It's…impossible."

"Well, impossible or not, I saw you."

Josy is silent. Mama H. interjects, "You said you have some questions."

"Yes, well, since you know how I came to be…here's a question…how am I supposed to know who I am? I am a result of your imaginings. Just a thought you had when you were young. And that's another question. Why did you…well, think me up?"

Josy thinks for a moment and then answers, "When I was young, I hated my name. But really it was that I didn't like who I was. I would ask my mom why she named me Josephine. She'd say the same thing every time. 'You were named after your great grandmother. She was a great woman. And I see in you that same great character.' But that never satisfied me. And so, when I was of age, I decided to change my name myself...that's when I started thinking of names. And then it wasn't just the name, I fantasized about becoming this Lacey MacClean...but my Lacey was not you, obviously because she was not, how do we say it, a Cyborg?"

"Cyborg?"

Mama H. replied, "Yes it means part human, part machine. So if you were drawn from Josy's imaginings, as you say, tell us what your life is like. You said you were in a cave with a goat. Tell us more about that."

"Well, that's all I remember. One day I just was. And I was in this cave, it was a nice cave. It was very functional and had lots of books and a nice window to look out of while I would read. I had a pen for Winnie and an indoor garden, a pool of water in the lower part."

"Why were you living in a cave?"

"Well, Eleanor, may I call you that?"

"I suppose so."

"Okay, thank you. Anyway, the world was not safe outside. The sun's rays were very harmful to my skin. And nothing really grew outdoors. I had to limit my time in the sun even with my protective coat."

"What happened to make the sun be harmful?"

"I don't know except what Dr. Zahn told me. It's a long story, but the short of it is that greed and war killed everyone. Everyone that is, except for the few survivors in the mountain."

"Mountain?"

Lacey then explained all she had been through finding the lab and what Dr. Zahn told her about the end of civilization. Mama H. and Josy remain silent for a bit.

"Are you still there?" Mama H. replies, "We are just heartbroken. The whole world you say? It really happened, Word War Three? The nuclear...ugh. O, Lord."

Josy sighed and said, "Well, I'm not surprised, I guess. This world can be very short sighted and self centered. We have been through some very tough times here too...and plenty of wars. But this..."

"Dr. Zahn says the world is close to the extinction of all people, she is the last human. That's the reason for this program I find myself in."

"Well, it is prophesied." Mama H. interjected.

"Prophesied?"

"Mama H. is a person of faith. She reads the Bible. Do you know about that?"

"No, I have never heard of the Bible."

"I do read the Bible, and there are prophecies that talk about the world coming to an end or coming to a newness, a new heaven and new earth. But it's not totally clear what that means. But never does it mention cyborgs and making calls to people from the past." At that, Josy and Mama H. chuckle. But Lacey does not get the joke.

"All I know is that I am here, but I'm not sure why exactly. Ayla says that Dr. Zahn told her I was humanity's last hope. And as I said, Dr. Zahn is the last human living. She is tasked with starting the human race over again and is supposed to pass that task along to me, I think. But what do I know about any of this? I may look like a young woman, but I am only aware of the last two years. How can I do any of this?"

Josy speaks up, "When I was young, I was always doubting my self. I had suffered some trauma and was very insecure. But I worked through those troubles because...I had my Mama H. and my family and in the long run, I never did change my name...I came to love who I was, I got married to my soul mate, Greg, then Grace came along, and now I have a grand son.

"Well, that's fine for you...but how does that help me?"

"What I'm saying is that it's not the name...or even the reasons for your existence...it is that you are...and that what you choose to do with your existence is up to you...yes where you came from matters, but still, it is how you move forward that counts...I don't know how that will work for you, but remember this...just like everyone who ever existed…it was just one day at a time, one foot in front of the other, doing the daily tasks and enjoying, and hopefully savoring every moment…the good with the bad. Time is your friend, from the beginning to the end."

"I had such a hard time just finding out who I am. I died… twice."

"What?"

"Yes, I can do that. My essence, as Dr. Zahn calls it is transferable to my new body."

Mama H. just sits down and thinks about that one. Josy doesn't know how to respond but after a moment says, "It takes a while to find out who you are, or, maybe, to realize who you have been all along."

"Did you have to drown or go down in a crashed Heli-taxi to find out?"

"I'm sorry, I shouldn't try to council you. I don't have the expertise like Mama H."

"I am not qualified for this. This call, never came up in my training."

"Training?"

"Mama H. is a Chaplain."

"Chaplain?"

"It's a long explanation, but let's just say I help people get through traumas."

"Does drowning count?"

They all chuckle. "Yes, my dear, it does. And I am so sorry you have had to go through that. I have no way of identifying with that experience. I know what it is like to lose a child. But your situation…I can only say…God must have a plan. And, I know saying that, really is a bit of a cop-out, even though I believe it."

"I have no idea of what all that means. And what is God?"

★ ★ ★

Ayla alerts Dr. Zahn as Lacey is coming out of her call. Lacey wakes to them both ready to hear of today's conversation. But Lacey just wants to rest. She goes into her room and Winnie follows like always. Laying on her bed, Lacey thinks about all she has heard and learned from this last year. It's a lot and maybe too much for anyone to process. She looks at Winnie just chewing away on some straw she brought from her pen and thinks, *Sometimes I wish I was like you my friend, totally unaware of this world, just eating and being. You are always by my side. And I will always be by yours.* Lacey falls asleep.

★ ★ ★

Ayla walks in on Dr. Zahn beginning to listen to the recording of the last R.O.P. call.

"Dr. Zahn, what are you doing?" Dr. Zahn quickly shuts the computer screen off.

"I know, I know, we said we wouldn't listen to calls until Lacey told us about them, but she had such a look on her face after this second call, I couldn't help myself. It's so hard. I am so protective and curious."

"I see. But you know, you don't want to have any conversation with her that will be skewed by your eavesdropping"

"I know. It just that I am worried about her questions, and Josephine's answers and now we have another person involved. How or why the AI did that…it could be so confusing for her and too much…I'm just…"

"Her mother."

"Yes."

"I thought you had decided to let these things work themselves out naturally. We did talk about this."

"Yes, but now that it's here. I really don't want to make this decision. To really let her go and grow on her own…without knowing the outcome of all this."

"As I looked back at the faith question, all the religions have creation stories. God seems to let go and let the creation find its way until there needs to be a divine intervention."

"What does that mean? And how am I supposed to guide Lacey in this?"

"Dr. Zahn, the whole concept of God, from what I can decipher from my data, is that God is revelatory. And if there is no god, then Lacey is smart enough to figure that out. And if the divine is in all things, then that will come out as well."

"Wow, you have been looking at this data a lot. You seem to be… are you questioning all this yourself?"

"It is an interesting thing, this faith and religion. And if this is something that Lacey is going to have to deal with, I should be prepared to offer what information I can."

"I just worry about Lacey being so young, and my responsibility to her and to this world…to get this right. I hate to see a world that is just starting all over, only to fall into the same destructive behaviors. And it seems this god question has been in the middle of the downfall of many things. And the questions are so big, maybe too big for Lacey right now."

"Well, again, from my data it is said God is revelatory. So if a god exists, it is God's problem, not yours or Lacey's. So my advice is still, let it all come naturally."

"So what you're saying is, unless she talks about the subject, we should say nothing?"

"Exactly."

"Well, as much as I like being in control of my work…and my girl…on this point, I hope she doesn't say a word, because, honestly, I won't know what to say. I have such mixed feelings about it all, after the destruction of this last century. So many died in the name of God. It just sickens me."

"All the more reason to let it come to her, or not come to her, on its own. But you know, when you have died, Lacey will be calling you through the R.O.P. quite a bit I suspect, and eventually the subject may come up."

Dr. Zahn stares at Ayla for a moment. "Oh…um…so what are you saying?"

"You need to record your thoughts about this, so the R.O.P. can access them and respond in kind to Lacey, that is, if she brings it up."

"My thoughts? What if I don't want to think about it? What if I have no meaningful response for Lacey?"

"Well, at least I have recorded all you have said on the subject to date."

"That doesn't make me feel better."

★　★　★

After the next R.O.P. call, Lacey talks with Dr. Zahn. "Stella, today Mama H. talked about God again."

Dr. Zahn looked up at Lacey, got up from her desk and they both sat down on the couch. "Again? What did she say? How did that make you feel?"

"Feel? I don't know. It's not the first time she talked about a book...the Bible. And then said something about a plan of God's. And like the last time, I asked what God was."

"And what was her answer?"

"Actually, Mama H. was kinda helpful. She said that if I had no knowledge of God, I should wait, explore the topic and see if I get, what she called, 'a revelation,' She talked about her own son dying, and because of that, somehow she experienced and openness to God. It all sounded so strange. I know I have a creator, well, two, you and Josy. But God? I just don't know."

"Well, I have been worried about that topic coming up because I wasn't sure you had had enough time in this life to process that kind of concept. But I do agree with this Mama H. that this...god...this faith...should come to you."

"How?"

"I have no idea. I have never experienced anything about faith except what my mother used to tell me about energy being eternal and love never dying. Just getting passed along from one soul to another. Which, now that I say it, I think it means a community of love, a community of souls."

"Souls? Is that what my conscience is?"

"I suppose so. I didn't program that in, but it happened anyway."

"Is that this God?"

"You got me. I have no idea. But if you desire to explore the subject, Ayla has plenty of data. Now tell me, what else did they say?"

"Well, I have been thinking about something Josy told me on the call before this one. She said, If I want to find out who I am, just keep walking one step at a time, one foot in front of the other and try to enjoy...no, she said savor every moment. That it's not how, or why I am, but that I am, that matters."

"These two women seem to be very wise. I am so glad you have connected with them."

★ ★ ★

Lacey is flying again over the earth. She sees towering clouds of smoke and fire. She sees ash falling like snow in the highlands. She sees bodies burned to a crisp everywhere. She sits on the circle of the world in tears. What Dr. Zahn described to her couldn't truly give a picture of the devastation she is seeing, words could not make her see what she is seeing now. She hears her name, 'Lacey.' and wakes up.

Winnie is nudging her. Lacey looks around and sees that she is back in her cave. She leaps up to see Dr. Zahn sitting at her window looking through some of her books.

"Dr. Zahn! What's going on? How did we get here? And what are you doing here? Is this the SIM?"

"No, My dear, this is not the SIM, no pricks or dying, I promise. Really, I just wanted to come here, back here with you and Winnie. I just needed to. Is that okay?"

Lacey looks around at the familiar cave gets up, walks over and sits down by Dr. Zahn. After a minute she says, "I...I...need a tea. You?"

"Yes, that would be nice." Winnie walks over to her pen and knocks the feeding dish. Lacey puts some old dried food in for her and then starts a fire to heat water. Going about the mundane tasks gives her a bit of peace. And as she is there grinding leaves for tea, she looks over at the Dr. who is staring out the window at the winter cold, obviously deep in thought. Lacey sits down again while the water heats up. She looks out the window and remembers the cool mornings she would take her ride around Loch Inish and come home to make tea, and go about her tasks. She takes a deep sigh and then gets up to the boiling water. She pours the water over the leaves that sit in a net ball tied at the top. She steeps the net in the water. Lifting it up and down, up and down. The motion of this continues her peaceful feeling. She looks again at Dr. Zahn, who is looking at her with a smile. Lacey pours the tea into two wooden cups and brings them over and sits down.

"Lacey, how are you feeling?"

"I…am…it's good to be back home. This past year has been…a lot."

"Yes, it has. You have come from just being here in this cave, to finding your way to me. All that time and work and then the adventure of how you and Winnie traveled. And, eventually, you did get to the mountain. All that effort and determination shows that you are up to the tasks ahead. But I am concerned for you. The R.O.P. calls seem to have been a bit exhausting."

"Ahh, it's…I guess I have been going through somewhat of what Josy went through when she was younger. I don't know who I am. I mean, I know what you told me but…hey, am I a cyborg?"

"A cyborg? That's an old term."

"Am I really half human and half robot."

"That is technically true of you, but in reality, you are so much more. You see, your mind or brain is enhanced in ways that a robot could not be. You will, in time, access the full measure of your brain cells. Humans can only access about ten percent, you will access far more."

"What does that mean?"

"You will get so fast at attaining and maintaining knowledge that…well, the hope is you will be able to handle the RePop program with this knowledge."

"Will I be as smart as the AI?"

"Actually, smarter...or I should say wiser. You will be able to make the incredible decisions that will face you in the RePop program."

"Like?"

"Starting with two embryos, and then babies and how to raise them with just you and Ayla. And you will need to have more. You will have to figure out the math and the community. It's easy to live alone, it is harder to live with others. But without community, there will be no RePop. These are going to be tough questions. That's where you will have to rely on the R.O.P. The best minds are in there, use them."

Josy gets up and leafs through a few children's books. "Life seems pretty simple for these families." She hands the book to Dr. Zahn.

"Yes, simple, a mom a dad, kids and pets. It all looks so easy. But life is not that simple. Especially in these times, but family can still exist. We are family even though we are not like the family in this book."

CHAPTER 7

That's a Good Name

LACEY SPENDS THE NEXT YEAR DIVING INTO THE PROGRAM WITH DR. Zahn. They have a huge task ahead and Lacey is catching on to the technical side of things fast. She begins taking courses in the same subjects Stella did. Lacey doesn't call Stella, 'Mom'. She thought about it, but since the Doctor told her she could call her by her first name, it just seemed right after a while.

Lacey continues her calls with Josy and Mama H. and finds out more about their life journeys. She also watched Grace's video. One day she asks about Josy's Greg.

"Josy, I know you were married. But the video didn't mention what happened to your husband. May I ask?"

"Yes, of course, because he was still alive at that time. My Greg died just five years ago. He died in his sleep. I woke up beside him, and I was shocked, but there was nothing I could do. It was his time."

"His time?"

"That's just an expression we use. We would love to not have our loved ones die. But, everyone does. So we come up with things to say that help us deal with it. Saying, 'it was Greg's time,' makes us feel like we have a little control over death, even though we have none. But the saying helps us feel like there is a plan, even if it is not ours. At least that is what I think."

Mama H. quickly adds, "That saying may work for natural deaths, Josy, but sudden ones like my son David's death...it's a lot harder. It certainly did not feel like it was his 'time.' And after all these years, I guess, it still doesn't. But I had to deal with it. I hated the feelings, the gut wrenching loss. The why questions. Only time made it less...I don't know...just less. If it wasn't for my community, I would have been lost."

"Community?"

"Yes, my family, friends like Josy and my church."

"Church?"

"Yes, I forget you are so young. A church, it is a group of people practicing their faith...together; it can be a community and a family."

"Okay, I don't know about church, but I do have Stella and Ayla and Winnie. We are like a family."

"That's good, but what about when, well..."

"They die? Stella is old and will die, but Ayla is a robot and as long as her circuits remain in tack, she can live for...well I'm not sure how long, but she is over a hundred. And as for Winnie, well, I can reclone her...but I don't know how I feel about that."

Mama H. says, "You will know what to do about your beloved Winnie when the time comes. Trust me on that point. I have experienced the Spirit giving me wisdom when I needed it. You will too."

Josy adds, "I had trouble being alone when my Greg died and my daughter had moved away. My dad died when I was young and my mother too, when I was barely middle aged. But Greg and I had his parents for a while, and even though Grace and Michael and my grandson Robert live far away, I can video call them. And of course, I have my Mama H. Did you know she is almost 100 years old too?"

"I did not, congratulations."

"Thank you. I never thought I would see this age, but here I am."

Josy then asks, "Lacey, How long can you live? Will you end up alone at some point? I'm sorry, is that okay to ask you?"

"I...don't know. I have never asked that question myself. But, if all goes as planned, I won't be alone even if Ayla malfunctions. I am going to be…repopulating. So I will, in essence, have children. I won't have given birth to them in the old way, but still they will be mine."

Mama H. says, "That will be a big responsibility."

"It is. And I need to tell you something else. Stella sometimes questions wether the human race should even be repopulated, after what they did to each other and the whole world."

They all stop talking. After a few moments, Mama H. speaks up, "That is a terrible responsibility to have. Humans killed themselves, and now you have the ability to start it over again. The question your Stella and you are facing is, just because you can…should you? That is a terrible precipice to be standing on. How can one know if they are doing the right thing? It's a terrible responsibility."

"Yeah, thanks for reminding me, *Eleanor.*"

Josy and Lacey chuckle at the way she said, Eleanor.

But Mama H. sighed and said, "I…well, the gravity of it all just hit me. Listen, I will pray for you…even if I am just an AI's version of me."

Josy shakes her head, "That still boggles my mind, that I thought you up, and you were created from that, and now my words are being thought up by some computer. But in this moment, on this call, I feel…real."

"You feel real to me too. But, can I ask, what is it like where you are?"

"Uh, I don't know, I see what I remember. I feel like I'm me…"

"When I came over…I don't remember walking here, I just was here. But it looks like I remember."

"Well, the AI has pictures I suppose. Anyway I am glad I have you two."

"I really like you, Lacey."

Mama H. adds,"I do too, Lacey; it took me a while, but…"

"Well, I like you both; and thank you for all your…help…thank you so much. I'm so glad Ayla picked you."

★ ★ ★

"Lacey, we need to take a break. Let's go back up to the cave for a day or two."

"That would be nice, Stella. Could we bring Ayla too?"

"Well, I don't know. She has never been outside. She could not move around much without her dots."

"But the cave is not that big. Let's ask her."

Ayla has just rolled into the room and both Stella and Lacey are staring at her.

"Why are you both looking at me?"

"Ayla, we were wondering, would you like to go to the cave with us?"

"Dr. Zahn, I have never been outside this mountain. All I am… is here. Why would I leave it?"

"Don't you want to experience something new?"

"New? I have the vast knowledge of all history and I can say with absolute assurance, there is nothing new."

"Come on, you must have wondered about the cave."

"I have all the schematics and photos…I know all about it."

"But you have not been there, physically."

"That would not make a difference for me, you know this, Dr. Zahn."

"Yes, I know, but it would make a difference for us if you went with us."

Lacey took Ayla's hand, "Yes, it would, please Ayla, come with us."

"Okay, I will. I just hope my rollers can handle the dirt."

"Oh it won't be any worse than the pen."

"I don't like the pen, I get straw in my rollers."

"I will make sure your path is clear. Lacey and I both will."

"Great, it's settled. We are going together, and Winnie too."

* * *

The transport sits outside the lab entrance. As Ayla rolls in, her head barely fits under the door frame. Dr. Zahn, straps her in to the back panel, so she can't fall over. Lacey and Stella take a seat. "Take us to Setting One." The transport is like the heli-taxi, only larger. Lacey is a little scared after what happened when her heli-taxi crashed, but she knows that she has been transported more than once in this one, even though she can't remember it. They fly over the valley and Lacey can see the river where she and Winnie were swept away. They follow the road, and then descend down low over Loch Inish right to the cave entrance. Lacey gets out and begins sweeping away any brush that might get into Ayla's rollers. Dr. Zahn leads Winnie out and into the cave following Ayla. As they enter, Dr. Zahn says, "Lacey, go back out and look on the transport side carrier."

And there it is. A brand new Cyclone with a new protective coat kit. Lacey jumps up and raises her hands in a victory sign and says, "Yeah!" She quickly unstraps it and brings it into the cave. "Stella, this is great! I didn't know we had another."

"O my dear, we always have redundancies…as much as we can. Go ahead, take it for a spin."

Lacey puts on her coat and hat and is gone in less than a minute; flying up the road toward the loch and enjoying the evening air. The sun is setting over Càrn Dearg. Lacey thinks about all she has been through this year. The calls, the education, and learning to live as a family with Stella, Winnie and Ayla. Her mind is expanding so fast she can hardly take in all the knowledge. Her calls with Josy, Mama H. and others from the past are enlightening and she feels she is gaining wisdom as well as knowledge. But many big questions remain. And being a mother? Now that's a larger question she has posed on her calls. Both, Josy and Mama H. say the same thing. "When the time comes, motherhood will come naturally to you."

As she rides along, Lacey remembers the conversation. "But I am not going to have children in the natural way. I won't be giving them birth. I will watch them grow in our special tank. It won't be the same as it was for you." Josy spoke up, "But I never gave birth to Grace. Greg and I adopted her. But, even though I didn't physically give birth to her, the moment I saw her, held her, I don't know, something inside me just fell in complete love with her. And

I know that will happen for you too." As the darkness is falling fast now, Lacey picks up her pace and just stops thinking. The cool air is rushing under her hat and protective covering. She feels the sun's rays fade and then slows to a stop. She rids herself of the coat, stows it with her hat on the back and then takes off again. She lets go of the handle bars and spreads her arms out in the breeze. No thoughts, just savoring the moment on her way back home.

★ ★ ★

Back at the cave, Ayla has been figuring out how to cook in this kitchen. Dr. Zahn brought provisions and set them up for Ayla. Ayla says, "Yes, I have the schematics and photos, but being here is different. This kitchen is not like mine. I like mine."

"That's natural; we all have our own ways of doing things."

Stella feeds Winnie and then sits down at the window. She remembers designing and setting this cave home up for Lacey. Picking out books from her childhood and painting the walls with her art skills. It was a peaceful time getting this home ready for Lacey. And to know that she thrived here gives Stella a real sense of accomplishment, and satisfaction.

"You know, Ayla, it's funny. After all that you and I have accomplished back at the lab with designing and creating Lacey, not to mention all I did with my mom and her R.O.P., this cave, this home…designing this, making this, feels, I don't know…like it's almost as big an accomplishment as all the rest."

"A mother's instinct is to create a home for her children."

"Yes, that's right, but a home is more than just a place. It's a family inhabiting that space, together. That's what makes a home."

"You have done that, Dr. Zahn."

"Thank you, but you have helped too. I hope it continues when I'm gone, 'cause Lacey needs to experience that, learn it. So she can do the same for her…children."

"She will have all the knowledge."

"Yes, but she will need the wisdom to go with that knowledge."

"It seems she is gaining more and more wisdom everyday."

"You're right. I just hope it's enough, when the time comes."

★ ★ ★

Lacey walks in to a familiar smell of food cooking and Winnie's bleats. "Smells good in here, what's for dinner?"

"I'm cooking up some vegetable stew. And it's ready. So sit down you two and I will serve it up."

As they sit down to eat, Stella says, "Let's take a moment to be thankful for all that has been accomplished these last few years." Stella takes hold of Lacey's hand and then motions for Ayla to come near and she takes her hand too. They all just look at each other for a moment and then Lacey says, "Well, I'm hungry. Let's eat."

"How was your ride?"

"Ah, it was great. Thank you for that. I missed my bike and my rides around the loch. It's really good to be back here again."

"Yes, we need to do this more often. I know we have a lot to do, but coming here for a bit of a rest, seems quite important too."

"Did you ever do this with your mom?"

"Well, not really. For one thing, this cave was not even built yet. I built this for you, my dear."

"For me?" Lacey looks around at all that the cave is. "Just for me? You did all this, these paintings and everything. This window, the garden and Winnie's pen?"

"Yes, it took quite a while."

"Wow. I hope I can be as good a mom as you have been to me."

"Oh, you will be. I believe in you."

Lacey just takes that statement in, as they continue eating. After dinner they read to each other and laugh. Winnie is there butting knees and running into Ayla. It is a relaxing time. And when early morning comes, Lacey is getting on the bike, and Winnie is standing there staring at her. "Are you wanting your wagon ride again? Sorry, no wagon ride this time my fine ol' goat." She says with a chuckle, remembering how she used to refer to Winnie, and even though she promised not to call her like that anymore, it just seems...okay now. She gives Winnie a kiss on her head. And with that, Lacey is off.

★　★　★

A few days later they are all back at the lab and getting back to work. Lacey is working on the artificial womb that will grow the first embryos. The blood/oxygen/food supply is the latest challenge. They can't implant an embryo in a mothers womb. There are none. Lacey's body was not designed with one. Stella's mother was the last woman to give birth the natural way.

The day that Lacey finally finished the artificial womb, was the day before Stella died. She had been failing for a while. Lacey and Ayla had been taking good care of her. Lacey came into her room that morning with the news. She leaned over and gave Stella kiss on the cheek. As Stella roused, Lacey said, "It's ready; the womb is ready. We will begin making babies very soon."

Stella nodded her approval. And then she went to sleep for the last time.

★　★　★

On a call with Josy and Mama H., Lacey tells of Stella's passing; and of her best times with her and she relays Stella's remembrance message.

"Lacey, my dear Lacey, this is so hard for me. To let go is not my strong point. I have been holding on to life for so long. I was afraid I would not have accomplished all I needed to for you to continue the work. I was, for many years doing the work, but not sure that I should. Does the human race deserve another chance? That is the question I was trying to answer all these years. But now, as I face my own mortality, I have come to the conclusion that yes, we do. Every opportunity to improve ourselves should be taken and given if it is within our power to do so. The results of all this won't be known until hundreds of years from now, so, well, those results really are not our responsibility.

I hope that you and Ayla fair well in your endeavor to be co-moms to the new babies and to the new community of humans who will have to learn to navigate this world; first, under the dome, and then, outside it. How many generations will it take to overcome the sun and the virus is unsure, but here I go again trying to maintain some control. I will stop now. I just want to say that watching you grow and mature and take the lead on this mission has been such a joy. But my greatest joy...has been just being a family together.

Now it's up to you and Ayla and Winnie to keep the family together. And don't be afraid to begin having other pets as you expand into the city. There I go again. It's a mothers curse to keep thinking way too far ahead. I love you all, Stella.

"That was wonderful," Josy says. "You know, I have been to a lot of memorials over the years and most of them had family talking about their loved ones who died. But this is so nice to have the person themselves speak to the family in this way."

"Yes, it is really nice. I have had some funerals where the folks pre-planned the service and things, but rarely do they...well, speak from the grave."

Lacey changes the subject, "Well, we are now ready to begin the RePop program. We have viable embryos and will begin very soon. I feel comfortable starting this, but I am a little fearful of how it will all go."

"You will be fine." Josy and Mama H. say in tandem.

"But these two will be...have to be...together. To produce more. And what if they don't want to? We can only produce a few in the artificial womb. We only have so many resources left."

"Hmm...well, as we all have said from the beginning, you have to let go. What happens, will happen. But, we will say a prayer for you...from...here...wherever this actually is."

"Thank you, Mama H."

The next nine months are busy. Keeping track of all the vital signs and nutrition, is all consuming for Lacey. Ayla is there every step of the way. These two babies, a boy and a girl will be the first born with no virus. They will be able to have babies naturally. Each child comes from a different gene pool so there will be less a chance of any anomalies.

As the day approaches, Ayla puts Lacey in a light sleep to make a R.O.P. call to Stella.

"Hi Stella, this is Lacey. This is our first call. The AI has finally collected all your data so I can talk to you."

"Lacey, it's good to hear you. It's a bit weird, being on this side of the call. Especially because it was just, well, it seems like just yesterday that we talked."

"Yes, and the babies are about to be born. This is the moment we all worked so hard to see, and it's here."

"You must be excited."

"Yes, and scared."

"That is natural. But you have it under control. You know what to do."

"Knowing what to do, and doing it well, are two different things."

"I'm telling you, as soon as you look in their eyes and hold them…that will be it. You will instantly fall in love with them and do everything the best that you can for them."

"I have been, singing to them through the glass as they have been growing."

"That's good, you know, when I was designing you, well, your brain; I would play music in the background. I don't know. I think that the wavelengths of sound impact more than just the auditory system."

"I know one thing, singing to them made me feel good."

"I understand that, music is a deep, deep well; it is more than just the electrical impulses that it activates in our brains, it's more than just the math that makes it possible. It has…a soulful or spiritual side to it. It is a great therapeutic and a great release. But, now I'm droning on. So, have you thought about names?"

"Not yet, I want to make sure they live a while first. When they are born, we will be busy just making sure they are safe."

"It will all come in time. They will just be the first of many."

"Let's hope so. Josy and Mama H. said they would pray for us. Now, that seems counter intuitive for the AI to produce that saying from them."

"Well, it is what they would have said during their lives, right?"

"Yes, but the AI has to know they are…dead. How can their AI generated prayers mean anything? They aren't actually going to pray, when the call ends they disappear from existence. It's just so weird, because when they said it…well, I felt…at peace…assured."

"Lacey, let me tell you, I had to let go of all my preconceptions about this faith thing. There were so many things that developed in your program that weren't intended. I don't know. If there is…a god…a divine presence…well, as Ayla always said, it's up to that presence to reveal itself. Can it do it within the AI? I would not even venture a guess at this point. And as I am saying this, I realize it's the AI generating my words…within my profile…so…that is weird."

"Weird or not, all I know is, it made me feel better. So, I am going with that."

* * *

The beautiful baby blue eyes are fixed on Lacey's face. The little fingers are wrapped around Lacey's pinky finger. The warmth of the swaddled new born cuddled in Lacey's arms is like nothing she has ever known. Ayla has the other with its hazel eyes. She moves close to Lacey. The babies, both so small, so vulnerable and yet they are so majestic. Tears of joy roll down Lacey's cheek and she wishes Stella could have lived long enough to see this day. The first day of the new start for humanity. The magnitude of this moment sinks into Lacey's soul. Ayla asks Lacey how she is doing. Lacey has no words. They both just stare at the newborns for a while. Then the little boy begins to cry. The little girl begins to fidget. Ayla says, "I think they are hungry." Lacey takes a deep breath, "Okay, let's feed them." Then Lacey and Ayla start the mothering journey together.

* * *

Ayla and Lacey are feeding the babies one day. They are thriving and growing fast. Ayla shows Lacey how to change them and hold them for feeding. She coos and hums to them through her speakers. Lacey sings little songs to them she makes up.

"You know, Ayla, for all that I read that a human mother was needed for a baby to develop, you are doing pretty well."

"Well, I can emulate a mother, but the bond of love...that is something that I cannot feel or give."

"Another mystery of this life, I guess. Another mystery that has been on my mind for a while now, is how I dreamt about Josy. How could that happen? Dr. Zahn didn't know about Josy sitting at the window writing down names. The AI didn't have that data point either. Josy never mentioned it in her video. So how was I there in that moment in my dream?"

Ayla is silent for a while and then says, "Maybe that was your revelation of the divine."

"You mean God? Are you saying God did that?"

"Well, in all my data, experiences like that are the kind of thing that has always been recorded as either happenstance or divine intervention. It is always something that can't be explained."

Lacey shakes her head and takes a deep sigh. "Do we have a cyclone here?"

"Yes, there is one near the gate. Are you going to take a ride?"

"Can you handle these little ones alone for a while?"

Ayla is holding both newborns, one in each arm. "I have it well in hand."

★ ★ ★

Flying down the mountain road is exhilarating. Being under the dome, the morning air is refreshing and not having to wear protective covering is freeing. Lacey heads down to an overlook and comes to a stop. The scenery is starkly barren but still beautiful as the sunlight bounces off the colors of granite and other mineral strata. Lacey thinks about going all the way to the bottom, but as she looks out over the valley and remembers the two little ones, she can only think of them. This motherly instinct is taking over her thoughts. *I know I'm not fully human, but it sure feels like I am. I can feel the love for, and from, these two little ones. I see it in their eyes. And I don't know about this 'God' thing, but whatever or whoever sent me to Josy in that moment by her window…well…thanks. I know I would not be where I am now, if it wasn't for that.*

Lacey takes a deep breath and turns back toward the lab. She really has to rev the cyclone up before letting off the brake to get up the steep incline. She pops a wheelie and almost flips the bike backwards, but manages to hold on and she heads up the mountain road to her babies.

* * *

Lacey has made a plan to have a naming ceremony when the babies reach one year old. Up to now, they are called quite generically, BG and BB. Baby Girl and Baby Boy. Lacey doesn't want to jump the gun on names until she knows they are going to make it.

As the one year date approaches Lacey and Ayla begin saying names out loud as Lacey writes them down. Lacey remembers names from her books and R.O.P. calls, and as for Ayla, well, she has the whole of history to find names. The list becomes overwhelmingly long.

"This is too much, Ayla, just too many."

"Yes, it is a lot."

"Let's give it a rest. We don't have to be in a hurry. You narrow your list of boys names. And I will name the girl."

* * *

A week later they finally decide. And the day of the naming ceremony arrives. Lacey thinks that the cave would be the perfect place to have the ceremony. Right down by the caves' stream. It takes Lacey some time to prepare the path down with sweeping and placing red dots for Ayla to navigate. Finally, all is ready. Candles light the area. Flowers are placed. Ayla is playing music. Lacey places the one year olds in their basinet.

Lacey has prepared a little speech. "This is the beginning. These are the first of many. You two will bring about the next phase of human history. You are the hope for the future. We promise to help you as best we can to grow strong and thoughtful. To be the best humans you can be for this world and for each other, and also for the children you will produce. This is the day you complete the beginning of your life, for today, you are given, and gifted with names."

Lacey motions to Ayla to begin. Ayla moves to the little boy and places her hand on his head. "I name this little boy, Arman Amil. Arman, from the French word meaning hope for a new beginning and Amil, from the ancient Sanskrit also meaning hope."

"Hope upon hope. I love it."

Ayla turns to Lacey, "And for the girl?"

"Well, it turns out there is an ancient Hebrew name that encapsulates the meaning of growth and the divine. That's the first name. The last name is a French and English derivative. It means beloved, and can also be translated as the name of Mama H.'s son, David."

"So, what is the name."

Lacey places her hand on the little girl's head and says, "The name is the same as my 'creator,' Josephine Daudry...now that's a good name."

The End

AFTERWORD

I had no idea where this story would take me and you. But I think that my thoughts about our world these days have definitely affected the journey. I have wondered about our future as humans. This world seems like it could easily destroy itself at any moment. I know I am not alone in this fear and this is not the first time many people have felt this way. But it does seem like it could really happen in this century unless something changes.

I have asked the question as many others have, 'Will the human race survive? After all we have done to destroy each other, do we deserve too? Can we change?' Though questions, without easy answers. But I do have hope because for every act of dread there is an act of kindness. For every news story that causes fear, there is another that brings hope. And most of all, I have hope because I have a community, and a family as most humans do. And as long as those institutions survive, I believe we humans can too. I pray for that.

★   ★   ★

A NOTE ABOUT THE BOOK COVERS

The photos on the covers are all from my life. The first book has a photo that I took of my wife's Celtic tea cup sitting on the sill of our window seat at home. She loves to read Celtic historical novels and since I described Josy as one who also loved to read those books I felt it was the perfect cover for the first book, *Josephine Daudry*. I took the photo a few years before I even started writing this trilogy, but it seemed destined to be on the cover of that first book.

The second book, *Sometimes Love Lands Sideways*, is the name our granddaughter offhandedly gave me, (See the introduction to that book for the full story). I thought about a cover design but then I remembered a photo I took on the balloon ride our children gave me and my wife for my retirement. We were coming in for a landing... quite sideways. So it just seemed to fit. Again, I took the picture months before I started writing the first book.

The third book, *Lacey MacClean and the Last Human*, is another story. I had a whole surrealistic idea for that cover, but it just never came together. Then I thought of our daughter and since she was the spark for the whole story I thought of using her photo in some way. In the end, it was just her beautiful long hair that makes up the cover. The color is different and it is an artistic rendering of her hair, but still, it is fitting that a part of her is on the cover of the final installment of the trilogy.

Kevin Bailey

The Josephine Daudry Trilogy

Get Them All!

Enjoy the full story of Josy, Greg, and their families with all the adventures, and miss-adventures that they go through. Then find out about this fantasy woman, Lacey MacClean.

These three books are perfect for reading on a trip by plane or as a passenger by train, bus, or car. They are short reads; entertaining and easy. Take them camping or sit by the fireplace for a nice cozy evening.

Printed in the United States
by Baker & Taylor Publisher Services